"Doesn't your job ever make you yearn for a child of your own?"

Vincente's unexpected question threw Rachel, so that she blurted out emotionally, "More than anything in the world." She added, "In due time, of course."

"That could mean anything from a few days to fifty years."

"Well, you can't have a baby without first having a husband!"

Deep, full-bodied laughter filled the plush interior. "You must be the last of an endangered species."

Dear Reader,

When I went to school in Europe, I absolutely fell in love with Spain, a country teeming with life and drama. The beauty of the people, the richness of the soul-stirring music, the aura of history hovering over every monument and city reached out to me, haunting me until I had to write about it.

In *The Baby Business*, I've tried to capture the essence of Spain by seeing it through the eyes of Rachel Ellis, a lovely young woman who meets the unforgettable Vincente de Raino and dares to dream of earthshaking love, of having Vincente's baby and of a future with him in a country which has taken her heart by storm.

Rebecca Winters

THE BABY BUSINESS
Rebecca Winters

Harlequin Books

TORONTO • NEW YORK • LONDON
AMSTERDAM • PARIS • SYDNEY • HAMBURG
STOCKHOLM • ATHENS • TOKYO • MILAN
MADRID • WARSAW • BUDAPEST • AUCKLAND

ISBN 0-373-03362-1

THE BABY BUSINESS

Copyright © 1994 by Rebecca Winters.

First North American Publication 1995.

Printed in U.S.A.

CHAPTER ONE

RACHEL ELLIS carefully negotiated the curves of the private mountain road, intent on her destination. Ordinarily she would have braked to admire the luxuriant foliage, but her need to locate Brian blotted out all other considerations.

Fortunately a worker near the gate volunteered to show her where she could find the *patrón*. While he ran ahead, she followed him past the stable to the paddock where she stopped the car and got out.

No one had to tell her which of the three black-haired men dressed in work pants and sweat-dampened white shirts was the owner of the magnificent estate she'd just entered. Finally she had caught up with the only person who might be able to lead her to her brother.

A number of impressions flew at her at once, particularly the attention and reverence the stable hands paid the hard-muscled male who stood half a head taller than the rest. Even at a distance, he moved with intrinsic masculine grace that set him apart from the other men.

He appeared to be discussing the merits of a high-spirited stallion racing around the enclosure. Whatever he was saying in Spanish held the stable hands' attention, but Rachel's background included only a little French, and though she could catch some similarities in words from both languages, she would never have been able to follow his conversation.

In fact, since arriving from New York the day before at Seville's San Pablo airport, everything felt foreign. It was so hot and humid she knew it would take a few days to acclimatize. She'd lost time waiting in line to pick up a rental car, only to discover that the air conditioner had gone out. The brutal ninety-nine degree August heat had depleted her strength, and today seemed even hotter, if that was possible.

Although her hair was caught back at the nape, perspiration bathed her skin, causing the silvery blond tendrils to cling to her damp forehead. The sleeveless, pale blue cotton blouse and skirt that had seemed so modest and appropriate when she'd put it on in her hotel room in Carmona earlier that morning now clung to her slender curves and long legs like a piece of wet gauze. But she was too upset about Brian to be concerned over her appearance.

She'd spent most of the day asking for directions to an obscure monastery in the Sierra Morena. Everyone nodded when she said the word "monastery," and gave elaborate directions. Not until midafternoon did she come across the right one, only to learn the shocking news that Brian no longer worked there as a caretaker, and had moved on a long time ago.

The compassionate abbot had seemed to understand Rachel's pain and had written a man's name and place of business on a piece of paper, suggesting he would know the whereabouts of her brother. *Señor Vincente de Riano, Jabugo.*

Rachel had thanked the abbot and had driven another hour to the picturesque mountain village which she learned was famous for its *serrano* hams, one of Señor de Riano's many business interests. But again she was destined to be disappointed because the owner had already gone home for the day. Rachel had had no choice but to return to Carmona and come back in the morning when his office opened at ten.

After consulting her road map, she'd started to follow the loop back to Seville. But her anxiety over Brian had grown so acute, she'd pulled to a stop in the next village and asked a local resident if he knew of the *señor,* if he could give her a home address or phone number.

The older man immediately nodded and pointed to a spectacular white villa clinging to the side of the green, wooded mountain in the distance. Rachel had thanked him, then had spent close to a half an hour trying to find the entrance to Señor de Riano's property.

A few feet closer now, she could see the surprisingly patrician lines of a face and body darkened to burnt umber by the relentless sun and how his black hair grew low on his strong neck, curling over his forehead in undisciplined abandon. Unconsciously she drew comparisons to Adonis, only this man looked as if the blood of the conquistadores flowed through his veins. She found him fascinating and caught herself staring at him, mesmerized by his unique male beauty and commanding air of authority.

Once, when he made an aside to the man on his left, Rachel glimpsed the unforgettable lines of his straight nose and strong jaw which lent character to his arresting features. She had the terrible premonition that in the future, she'd compare every man she met to *him*, and would find them wanting.

Not even Stephen whose exceptional looks masked a fatal flaw, could compare...

Perhaps this was how her mother had felt the first time she met Rachel's handsome father, a charismatic man who had an irresistible appeal for women. A man who couldn't remain faithful and who had left his wife and children to fend for themselves.

The *señor* must have sensed Rachel's approach because he turned in her direction, and the flashing black eyes which had been so curiously alive, immediately narrowed as his chilling gaze took in her darkly fringed violet eyes and the fine-boned oval of her face. She couldn't understand his reaction.

People meeting her for the first time often marveled at her unexpected coloring, yet this man seemed to find the combination repugnant. An implacable mask had slipped into place, depriving his features of animation when only seconds before he'd been in total harmony with his surroundings.

"Señor de Riano," she said, taking a tentative step toward him. *"¿Habla usted inglés?"* she asked one of the few questions she'd memorized in Spanish.

After a brief pause, there was an imperceptible nod of his dark head.

Though baffled by his frigid hauteur, she walked a little closer. "I'm Rachel Ellis. Forgive me for intruding this way, but I'm quite desperate to find my brother, Brian, and I understand you might know his whereabouts."

He made no move toward her, neither did the stable hands who stared at her with dark, incredulous eyes, as if they couldn't believe what they were seeing.

"Señor?" she prompted him, wondering after all if his English wasn't any better than her Spanish.

"You're even more audacious than your brother, Miss Ellis," he finally condescended to speak in clipped tones. "It seems you two share a great deal besides identical physical characteristics."

Surprised, she blinked. The abbot was right. This man *did* know Brian. Not only that, he spoke perfect English with only a trace of accent, delivering his insult in a low, cultivated voice full of icy contempt.

"I—I don't understand. You sound an—"

"No one is asking you to," he cut in on her brutally. "You and your brother have the distinction of being the only two..."

He stopped midsentence and one black brow lifted menacingly. "If he sent you here to plead his cause, then he's an even bigger fool than I'd imagined. Before I have you escorted back to where you came from, I want to know why you traced me to my home."

Rachel smoothed the damp hair away from her temples, not having the faintest idea what he was talking about, let alone why he would threaten her this way. His rancor ran marrow-deep, making her want to cry out at the unjust accusations. "Are you always this charming to strangers at a first meeting?"

His mouth thinned to an uncompromising line. "You didn't answer my question. I'll have the truth," he warned. As he started toward her, the other men dispersed and headed for the stable at her back.

Her first instinct was to retreat, but her bewilderment was fast turning to anger and she refused to let him intimidate her any further. "Because I need to find my brother and the abbot at the monastery near La Rabida told me you might be able to help me. A local villager indicated this was your villa and when I reached the gates of your estate, one of the workers kindly ran in front of my car to lead me to you."

His expression hardened, letting her know that bit of news had displeased him even more. His reaction prompted her to add, "Apparently he doesn't know that Brian and I manage to bring out the darker side of your personality. Please don't reprimand him for being courteous to a foreigner."

His mouth tautened. "It was probably Jorge who is more susceptible than most to a lovely face." His voice grated unpleasantly. "Be that as it may, you've wasted your time and your money. There are a half dozen flights to the States every day. I suggest you be on the first one leaving in the morning, *señorita*."

Dismissing her, he turned away and whistled to the stallion who made an answering snort and came flying across the paddock at his master's command.

"And I suggest you go to hell, *señor.*"

Rachel had never said such a thing to anyone in her life, but she'd never been so enraged before. "I haven't exhausted all my possibilities yet. If you've made Brian's acquaintance, then so have other people in the area. Someone will be able to help me."

Realizing how pointless it was to stay in this impossible man's presence any longer, Rachel spun around and headed for the car parked near the paddock.

"I wouldn't count on that," came the mocking retort.

Rachel slowed her steps and half turned to him, her cheeks aflame with indignation. "Don't try to intimidate me, *señor.* I'm not one of your terrified employees who is beholden to you for my livelihood."

His body stiffened and a tension-filled silence stretched between them. "Like your brother, you don't look before you leap. Just remember that you're in my country now, and we play by a different set of rules."

She lifted her proud chin mutinously. "What a delightful man you are. Were all your meetings with Brian this pleasant?"

"Let's just say they were memorable," he replied cryptically, "have no doubt of it." His eyes narrowed to inky black slits.

"What happened?" she said, relishing baiting him. "Did Brian suggest confession might be good for your soul? Did he advise you to pay a visit to your good friend, the abbot, in La Rabida?"

A wintry smile broke out on his bronzed face, allowing her a glimpse of what he'd look like if he were really smiling. Even so, she didn't want to admit the devastating effect.

"When was the last time you saw your brother?"

The question went straight to the heart of her pain, but she'd rather die than reveal any vulnerability around this forbidding man.

"It's been a while," she dissembled in what she hoped was a level voice.

"Apparently long enough to make you a believer of his lies."

"What lies? If anything, my brother is brutally honest, even if it hurts someone else." She stood her ground though it felt like she were suffocating in quicksand, and not just figuratively. The oppressive heat and humidity were fast making her feel not only sluggish but light-headed.

"That's quite a testimonial," he rasped.

She sucked in her breath. "That's because I know Brian, and his word has always been good enough."

"Perhaps it was, *once,*" he said pointedly, reminding her of her mother's words before she died.

I don't know if I trust your brother to tell us the truth about anything anymore, Rachel. He's been gone too many years, and I have this awful feeling about him.

Rachel had thought that her mother's doubts about Brian were a result of her own pain and disillusionment. But Rachel couldn't very well ignore this autocratic man's assessment of Brian.

Still, her first loyalty would always be to her brother who'd suffered from their father's desertion as if he'd been mortally wounded and had left home to drift around Europe in an attempt to blot out the pain. Rachel, two years older than Brian's twenty-four years now, had secretly grieved along with him but anguish had made her turn inward and she'd sought solace in tending other people's children.

How her boss, Stephen, had hated her preoccupation with her brother's absence, accusing her of being in permanent mourning, of loving her brother more than she loved him.

With hindsight, she wondered if he hadn't spoken the truth after all. Perhaps in the end, frustration over her inability to be heart-whole had led him to stray in other directions. Which didn't make the pain of his betrayal any easier to bear, or excuse his behavior. But it could conceivably explain it.

However, dwelling on the past wouldn't get her anywhere and she lifted her head. "Just answer me one question, *señor*. Have you seen Brian recently?"

His mouth twisted nastily. "No."

That one word dashed her hopes to pieces and she hurt with a pain so deep she couldn't separate it from all the other pain she'd endured. Rachel felt as if she'd come to the end of her life.

Through glazed eyes she stared at the imposing male. Evidently he'd formed such a negative impression of Brian that one look at Rachel with her blond Ellis genes, and he'd ordered her back to the States on the first available flight.

Dear God, what was going on with her brother? *Was* he in some kind of trouble?

That's what her mother had believed. If Rachel could see Brian right now, would all traces of the vulnerable boy-man—who at eighteen hadn't been able to leave New York fast enough—have disappeared?

No matter that six years had gone by, in any battle of the wills Brian would be no match against someone of Señor de Riano's mien. The man was not only older in years, but in human experience.

She brushed the perspiration off her forehead with the back of her forearm, trying to weigh everything carefully, but the setting sun still scorched her skin and made coherent thought impossible. Swallowing her pride, she said, "Then can you tell me where he is?"

"No."

"And you wouldn't tell me if you could!" she accused when nothing else was forthcoming.

After a lengthy pause he said, "Why have you come here, *señorita?*"

"That's my business, surely," she was stung to retort.

"I thought you were desperate to find him."

Her chest heaved, drawing his eyes, which made a sweeping male appraisal of her feminine attributes.

"I am."

"Did he send for you?" he asked, his voice steely.

Again, deep pain seared Rachel because never once in all the years he'd been gone had Brian suggested that they meet somewhere. She sensed that her interrogator thought otherwise, that he was vitally interested in her answer.

"No," she finally admitted, shaking her head which was a mistake. Everything swam before her eyes and when she started to weave, he made a lightning move to close the distance between them. He put a steadying hand on her arm, sending a shock wave of feeling through her body, a sensation she'd never experienced with another man, not even Stephen. Alarmed, she pulled away from him and he let his hand drop.

Something undecipherable flickered in the black depths of his eyes, making her more aware of his physical presence than ever. "But you came anyway."

"Yes." To her despair, tears beaded her dark lashes. *Damn.* She looked at the ground. "Our mother died unexpectedly of pneumonia." In an effort not to reveal emotion, the words came out on a wobbly whisper. She moistened her lips nervously because she could feel his intent gaze studying her features. "He doesn't know yet. The letter I sent to church authorities in Seville came back unopened."

Her grief had reached its peak when she'd seen the words *addressee unknown* scrawled in Spanish across the bottom of the envelope. She assumed it had been undeliverable because whoever was in charge hadn't tried hard enough to trace a lowly caretaker.

But Señor de Riano patently didn't believe her story. Fortunately she'd brought the letter with her in case she hadn't found her brother and had to leave it with a priest to give to Brian.

She'd written it right after her mother had been buried, pouring out her heart to Brian, expressing her tenderest feelings. All the anguish and grief she'd been suppressing came out in a torrent of emotion-laden words, and she couldn't put herself through the agony of writing another letter like that again.

"Here. Read it." Her unsteady fingers pulled the envelope from her tote bag. She handed it to him, hoping the proof might have a softening effect, at least enough for him to relent and tell her what was going on with Brian, how she might contact him.

He took the letter, but his penetrating eyes never left her face. "You're about ready to pass out from the heat," he said in a surprisingly husky tone, his earlier hostility not apparent. The next thing she knew he'd picked her up and carried her swiftly along a path which led away from the stable to the lush gardens at the back of the villa.

Though she never lost consciousness during the short walk, a wave of perspiration drenched her body and her ears hummed. She felt so lethargic, she couldn't find the strength to lift her head from his broad chest where his heart pounded steadily against her cheek and temple.

But she wasn't too far gone to register a brief, unfamiliar sensation of feeling safe and cherished in this man's arms. Again, her thoughts flew to Stephen who up until a few weeks ago had been the man she'd hoped to marry. How blind she'd been not to see that he had always played the injured party, expecting comfort from her!

It shook her that Señor de Riano should be the one to illuminate Stephen's selfishness with such revealing clarity. She couldn't fathom the dichotomy of emotions this arrogant stranger aroused in her.

They reached a covered patio with a colonnade of Moorish arches, decorated with blue tiles and overflowing with potted flowers. He deposited her on a lounger, and as if by magic a maid appeared. Within seconds her enigmatic host pressed a glass of something cold in her hand, urging her to drink. He stood close by with his powerful legs slightly apart. When she had finished, he took the empty glass.

Between the cooler temperature and the crushed lemon ice, she started to feel better. "Thank you," she murmured gratefully when he handed her another, then drained one of his own. She couldn't help staring at the strong column of his throat, the way his tanned, ringless fingers splayed around the glass. Their eyes met unexpectedly, and she experienced another wave of sensual awareness, much stronger this time. Her breath caught in surprise before she turned her head sharply away.

"Obviously your brother failed to mention that this area is called *La Sartenilla de Andalusia.*" Curiosity overrode common sense and Rachel ventured a guarded look at him. "In your language we are referred to most unattractively as the 'frying pan of Andalusia,'" he explained dryly.

Rachel could believe it, but wished he hadn't been witness to her heat exhaustion. Gathering her composure, she said, "I'm feeling much better now, thanks to you. Since you can't tell me anything more about my brother, then there's no need to disturb you further. If I could just have my let—"

"Not so fast," he said, cutting off her words. This time when she looked at him, he was studying the contents of her missive, then glanced at the May postmark stamped on the outside of the envelope. "Why did you wait three months if you were so eager to make contact with your brother?"

Why was he continuing to treat her as if she were some kind of criminal?

"Money. I had to settle debts and make sure I had some savings in the bank before I left because—" She stopped abruptly, not willing to reveal that she'd broken off with Stephen, which resulted in her being fired ten days before this trip.

Thank God she'd caught him out before they'd said their vows. Marriage to him would have been the greatest mistake of her life!

When she returned to New York, she would have to look for another job, which might prove difficult if Stephen refused to give her good references. Understanding his petty nature as never before, she realized he was vindictive enough to blame her for his own indiscretions and never do the decent or honorable thing where she was concerned.

"Th-the reason doesn't matter," she said, getting out of the lounger. To her chagrin, he watched with unabashed interest as her skirt rode up her thighs, revealing her shapely limbs. "I'm here now—" she barely got the words out, her cheeks flushed "—and I'll find Brian on my own."

She plucked the letter from his hand and started to leave the patio, but a hand of steel gripped her upper arm and prevented her from moving.

"When was the last time you saw him? No more evasion."

Rachel didn't understand the reason for his question and had trouble concentrating since all she could think about was the warmth of his fingers on her sensitive, bare skin. There was something incredibly intimate about the gesture.

"Six years."

"*¡Madre de Dios!*" He bit out an epithet and let her go. He raked a hand through his thick hair which had a tendency to curl around his neck and forehead. "He's no longer a boy."

She took a steadying breath. "Naturally we'll both have changed a great deal."

"Except that the two of you will always share the classic bone structure and hair color the people of my country worship."

"Yourself excepted," she blurted out, recognizing that he'd paid her a compliment of sorts, but that he still hadn't changed his opinion of Brian's character, or hers for that matter. Not waiting for a response, she headed for the garden, but only reached the first step before he blocked her way with his tall body whose warmth and scent held her in thrall.

"Where are you staying while you're in the province, Miss Ellis?"

She defied him with her eyes. "Does it matter?"

"*Sí, señorita*. It matters a great deal if you have a distance to drive. The roads are not safe after dusk, particularly not for a beautiful American woman who is alone and obviously quite defenseless."

She'd been told the same thing by the travel agency which had made her hotel and flight arrangements. An increase of thefts and attacks on tourists from the States and the UK had made her cautious and inwardly she was concerned about the drive back to her hotel.

Again this man of contradictions confounded her with his solicitude. When she thought back to Stephen, it occurred to her that never once in their relationship had Stephen ever worried about her safety away from him. He was too self-centered to look beyond his own needs.

What upset her now was that it took a man as exasperating as this Señor de Riano to make her see Stephen's many faults in their true light and put them in perspective. *How could that be?*

"I'm staying at the Del Rey Don Pedro in Carmona."

He studied her face with an unreadable expression in his eyes. "Considering the fact that a lack of finances kept you from coming to Spain until now, I find it strange that you would choose that hotel when there are many other hotels in the area less expensive."

Rachel could hear the suspicion in his voice and a fresh spurt of adrenaline surged through her body. "I was hoping Brian could take a few days' retreat with me in elegant surroundings since I know he's been deprived of so many creature comforts since he left home.''

"Prophetic words," he muttered beneath his breath but she heard him and couldn't take any more of his hateful treatment.

"What kind of man are you?" she cried out in anger and frustration. "You obviously know something I don't, and appear to enjoy baiting me like those poor bulls in the *corrida*. Perhaps cruelty is included in the makeup of your Spanish genes.''

His black brows met together in a distinct frown, making her inordinately glad because it meant she'd hit a nerve.

"Contrary to your belief, the Spanish don't have the monopoly on that particular trait. The Americans have been known to commit their own kind of atrocities. Your brother is a case in point," he retorted dangerously.

At the mention of Brian, a palpable tension hovered between them, filling her with dread. Rachel had an idea that this man's anger was personal, deeply personal, that Brian had wronged him in some unforgivable way.

Struggling for breath she said, "Whatever Brian has supposedly done, then I need to know what it is so I can talk to him, reason with him, and help him make restitution, if that's the case.''

His mirthless smile defeated her. "How very noble of you, Miss Ellis. However, your self-sacrifice comes far too late.''

Rachel blinked. "What do you mean?"

One brow quirked in derision. "You may very well ask. Your brother has gone into hiding for a crime which has put his partner in jail."

CHAPTER TWO

RACHEL SHOOK HER HEAD in denial and backed away from him until one of the columns stopped her. *"No,"* she whispered, remembering her sensitive brother who'd been a model son until their father had left, an act which had devastated all their lives. "It isn't possible. There has to be a mistake."

"I'm afraid not."

He must have noticed the blood drain from her face because once again she found herself being assisted to one of the chairs surrounding the patio table. Ironically enough, she was thankful for his support.

Brian was in hiding?

She couldn't comprehend it and lifted wounded eyes to him, unaware they'd gone a deep purple color. Her heart was in her throat. "He couldn't have killed someone."

Señor de Riano stood a few feet away, his arms folded across his broad chest. After an ominous quiet he said, "No."

"Thank God," she cried, fighting tears, but they streamed down her pale cheeks anyway. "I take it you're the injured party. What did my brother do to you?"

"It wasn't just to me," he growled in quiet menace, but she thought she detected a betraying tone of personal loss that tugged at her emotions and brought her head up.

He'd moved to the edge of the porch, his powerful body more in silhouette now that the sun had dipped below the horizon. With one bronzed hand propped against an arch, he stared out over a mountain landscape of massive oak, walnut and chestnut trees. More than anything else his stillness warned her that what she was about to hear would be ugly.

"A year ago—against my better judgment—I hired your brother to work at the plant in Jabugo and provided him with housing. He and another foreigner, a Swede, who'd asked for a job at the same time, roomed together and drew the same assignment in the packing and freight department."

Rachel dreaded to hear the rest and sat rigidly on the edge of her seat.

"Your brother came recommended by the abbot who said he was an honest, hard worker and deserved a better salary than the one the church could pay him. The abbot has been a family friend since I was a boy and I've always considered it an honor to grant him any favor. But where your brother is concerned, I'm afraid even the abbot was duped."

Her spirits plummeted. "What exactly did Brian do?"

"Within weeks of being hired, he and the Swede started stealing hams and sold them through the European black market for an exorbitant price. At first the people in shipping thought they'd been careless with their figures and had made a mistake. But in time there was a significant loss of inventory. Twenty thousand dollars' worth, to be exact.'' Rachel gasped at the amount. ''Five months later, the Swede was caught redhanded and arrested. The police traced his money to a Swiss bank account.''

''And Brian?'' The question came out in a tortured whisper.

''The day his roommate was taken into custody, your brother failed to report for work and there's been no trace of him since. That was six months ago.''

Dear God.

''The Swede made a full confession, implicating your brother from the outset.''

Unable to stand it any longer, Rachel sprang to her feet. ''That doesn't sound like the Brian I love. If you didn't catch him with the evidence, then you only have the other man's word. I can't believe my brother had any part in it. The abbot wasn't wrong!''

Her host stared mercilessly at her. ''Did your brother contact you? Did he tell you he was innocent?''

''No!'' she cried. ''I wish he had! Obviously you don't believe me, but if you knew Brian, you'd understand that he's always been too proud to admit when he was in trouble.''

Rachel buried her face in her hands, thinking back to his last phone call. ''He must have already left Seville when he phoned mother and me to tell us that we might not be hearing from him for a while,'' she murmured, her voice trailing. "Mother sensed something was wrong, but I didn't want to believe it."

She shook her head in despair. "I've got to find him and convince him to tell the authorities the truth. Where could he be?"

Señor de Riano rubbed the pad of his thumb along his lower lip, his expression unreadable. "My guess is, he's still in Spain."

"Why do you assume that?" She had an idea the *señor*'s opinion wasn't mere idle speculation.

"When a man wants something badly enough, it's amazing how tenacious he will be," came the response.

She bristled all over again. "What more could he want than exoneration?" Her cry reverberated in the perfumed air. "Look, *señor*—I'm not trying to minimize the gravity of this situation, but for all his faults, I don't believe Brian is guilty of anything more serious than not being able to come forward for fear he won't be given a fair hearing. He's in a foreign country and doesn't know the laws. If you were in his shoes and had no money, what would *you* do?"

He stared at her for an overlong moment. "You wouldn't by any chance be studying to become a solicitor?"

She'd had enough of his condescending mockery. "I'm afraid the law doesn't interest me to that degree, *señor*."

"Might I enquire what does?" He subjected her to another appraisal, more intense this time, as if he were searching her soul.

"My work is nothing impressive, but it's satisfying to me."

"Enlighten me, *por favor.*"

"I'm a hotel nanny."

Her revelation must have been the last thing he'd been expecting because his expression altered and his eyes gleamed with uncommon interest. She didn't like or understand that calculating look.

He paced the tile floor as if he were working out an intricate problem, then came to a standstill and stared at her. "You're licensed?" he persisted in the same vein.

"I could never be employed at the Kennedy Plaza without one." He'd made her defensive, and she couldn't hold back the sarcasm. She wondered what kind of a reaction she'd get if she told him about the awful scene with Stephen that led to his firing her, leaving her temporarily jobless.

But on second thought, she decided she didn't want to find out. "I—I know I don't earn a big salary, but I can make you one promise. Until Brian comes forward, I'll pay you back his supposed portion of the money in monthly installments."

With only one thought on her mind, which was to return to Seville and talk to the police about where to go from here, Rachel started down the porch steps leading to the flower garden. But she came to a standstill when he said, "You think that money alone can atone for his sins?"

Rachel whirled around, wondering if she'd understood him correctly. "What sins?" *Were there more?*

Like a dark prince, he stood tall in the deepening shadows. "Perhaps your brother should be the one to explain after all." He paused, making her more aware of the sound of crickets and the heavy fragrance of roses. "Night will be upon us soon. I'll follow you back to Carmona in my car, to make sure you arrive safely."

Rachel hated being in Vincente de Riano's debt for any reason, and she wanted to tell him that the gesture wasn't necessary. But he was no ordinary man and possessed a chivalrous streak which appeared to be a part of his complex makeup. Somehow she knew it would be futile to argue with him.

"As you wish, *señor*," she murmured, and hurried along the path of the extensive grounds to her car which was parked around the side of the villa.

By the time she had driven through the gates and had headed back to Seville, night was fast encroaching. Much as she hated to admit it, she felt secretly relieved that he was behind the wheel of the big black estate car she could see in the rearview mirror as she drove down the lonely mountain road. But because her turmoil ran so deep where Brian was concerned, she almost missed the N-4 turnoff for Carmona and was once again beholden to Señor de Riano who flashed his lights to alert her.

Obviously he hadn't told her the full extent of Brian's problems. Rachel couldn't help but wonder if the *señor* was being deliberately cruel in holding back certain information because he needed to strike out at the injustice which had been done to him.

Although if he were a deliberately vindictive person, he wouldn't have shown compassion when he saw she was suffering from heat exhaustion. Instead, he had carried her out of the sun to his villa to refresh her, arousing feelings of sensual awareness in her which even now had the power to make her tremble. She didn't think those were the actions of a man bent on retribution.

In fact, now that his last cryptic comment had finally started to sink in, she had the eerie feeling that Brian was in much deeper trouble than Señor de Riano had been willing to let on. A shiver chased over her skin, chilling her despite the warm night air.

Her feelings of apprehension heightened as she reached the massive, meters-thick walls housing her hotel located within the remains of the Alcazar de Arriba which was once the lavish palace of King Don Pedro and later became a refuge of Catholic kings during their final battle against the Moors.

She could easily imagine the *señor* in the role of a Spanish nobleman, capable of great passion whether in love or war. One who was forced to deal with the many covert intrigues of court life and mete out punishment upon those unfortunate souls who were unwise enough to merit his wrath.

Shocked at the extent of her errant thoughts, she tossed her head as if to rid herself of his image and pulled into the parking area next to the hotel. Her heart raced wildly when he followed suit and drew his car alongside hers. The low, purring sound of the motor reached her ears as she switched off the ignition.

Any hope that she could escape without further contact with him vanished as he got out of his car and came around to assist her.

"There was no need for you to accompany me," she reminded him in a defensive tone as she locked the car.

"I wonder what you would have done if the car with three men which started following you outside Aracena hadn't been put off by my presence and finally given up the chase a few kilometers back."

Her stunned gaze flew to his.

"*¡Por Dios!*" His expression was thunderous. "You didn't realize?"

"N-no." Rachel's heart started to thud sickeningly in her chest. To her consternation, her thoughts had been centered on *him,* blotting out everything else. If he hadn't stayed close by—

"Let's get you inside before you decide to faint on me again."

Heat swamped her cheeks. "I didn't faint on you, and I don't need your help, *señor.*" But he had already clasped her elbow in a firm grip. She fought unsuccessfully to ignore his touch as he escorted her along the path to the Moorish-styled entry, leaving the maze of narrow cobbled streets and whitewashed houses behind.

"I beg to differ. After all, if you're going to make restitution for your brother in his absence, then by all means I intend to keep you safe while you're in my country."

She hated his patronizing tone and had difficulty understanding why he would bother to help her to this extent when it was her brother he firmly believed had caused him such grief. She feared Señor de Riano's offer of assistance had sprung more from some ulterior motive than from chivalrous tendencies after all, and it made her more suspicious than ever of his unsolicited attention. But trying to separate herself from him got her nowhere.

"I assume part of your weakness stems from hunger," he said near her ear as he guided her through the vaulted dining hall to the adjacent bar with its brass lamps and wood-paneled ceilings. The fact that he was dressed in shirtsleeves and work pants only seemed to add to his attraction and drew the eye of every female they passed, young or old.

It would take an unusual man to handle that kind of attention for a lifetime and remain true to the woman he loved. In her limited experience, few men did. Of course, for all she knew the *señor* wasn't married, although from what she'd read, most Spanish men married early.

If that were the case, did he love his wife to the exclusion of all else, or like most men with an overabundance of sex appeal, *had he already abandoned her?*

Once again Rachel found those thoughts disturbing. "I'm afraid I'm too upset to eat anything and plan to go straight to my room," she remonstrated sharply in reaction.

But he'd already caught the attention of the wine steward who greeted Señor de Riano like visiting royalty and flew past the other guests to attend him with deferential smiles and a volley of unintelligible Spanish. Several times his admiring glance flicked to Rachel before he hurried back to the bar with the *señor*'s instructions.

"Relax, *señorita*." Her companion held out a chair from the table. "You've done all you can do for one day and would be wise to look after yourself."

"Is that a warning?" she blurted out hotly, uncaring of the other diners' interest.

"Take it any way you wish," came the dispassionate comment, underlining her fear that he hadn't told her everything.

Short of making a scene, she had little choice but to do his bidding, especially when a waiter had arrived at their table with a tray of shellfish hors d'oeuvres that made her mouth water in spite of her protestation that she wasn't hungry.

"In case you were wondering, these are called *tapas* and can be a meal in themselves. I trust you'll be able to find something to your liking while I make a phone call to the police. They need to be alerted that you are here and are anxious to cooperate."

He hesitated momentarily before walking away. She had the impression he'd mentioned the police as a deliberate ploy to provoke a reaction in her. But if he thought she'd try to stop him because she had something to hide, then he was destined to be disappointed.

A little smile broke the corner of her mouth. He noted it with a distinct grimace before his long strides took him from the room. Deep in thought, she didn't realize that the steward had returned with a brandy snifter full of iced juice, something similar to what she'd been given at the villa. *"¡Buen provecho, señorita!* Enjoy."

She murmured her thanks and cautiously sipped her drink. It turned out to be an unusual combination of lime and banana, lightly laced with alcohol. She thought she'd never tasted anything so good and after drinking most of it, reached for a shrimp *tapa* which melted in her mouth, making it impossible for her to stop at just one.

"I'm glad to see you took my advice," a deep male voice she was coming to know spoke from behind her. Suddenly what little appetite she had, fled, and she looked up at him anxiously. His taut, hard-muscled body stood uncomfortably close to hers, making her more nervous than ever.

"Do the police have a lead on Brian yet?"

His black eyes impaled her. "No, and for the present they require nothing of you except to know where you are staying while you are in my country. I've told them you can be reached here. Naturally they'll want to be advised of the date of your return trip to the States."

Her misery intensified. "I—I don't know that yet. I have an open-ended ticket because I didn't know how much time Brian would be allowed to take off to spend with me."

Taking a deep breath, and willing herself to stay composed, she wrote out several traveler's checks worth two-hundred-fifty dollars which she left on the table. The small sum of money bequeathed to her and

Brian upon their mother's death was diminishing fast. "This represents the first installment."

She avoided his probing glance as she pushed back the chair and stood up. He still didn't trust her and she couldn't help but anticipate the worst where Brian was concerned. How ironic that she'd flown to Spain for a reunion at a monastery and instead had walked straight into purgatory.

"Thank you for the information," she said, realizing that something was still expected of her; however, she hated having to acknowledge in any way that she needed or was grateful for this man's help. "If Brian should contact me, I'll let both you and the police know immediately. *Adiós, señor.*"

She hadn't gone three feet before she heard, *"Buenas noches, señorita."* His deliberate refusal to say a formal goodbye sounded faintly menacing and she hurried through the common areas to reach the long, castlelike corridors which led to her room overlooking the spectacular country to the south.

Once inside the door, she raced across the tile floor and flung herself facedown on the bed where she could give in to the emotions consuming her body. She'd never felt this alone in her life.

After her mother had died, she began spending more time with Stephen. Until that dreadful scene in his hotel room which had revealed his shallow character.

From the beginning, he'd wanted her to go to bed with him, but she'd put him off, telling him she preferred to wait until they were married, until she'd found her brother so he could give her away at the wedding.

At first Stephen agreed, but as time went on he grew more and more testy and difficult. After one particularly ugly quarrel over Brian, she decided she couldn't bear the tension any longer and decided to sleep with him, hoping to appease him. Summoning her courage, she got one of the maids to let her in his private suite unannounced, anxious to surprise him when he came off duty.

The surprise blew up in her face when she discovered him in bed with one of the nannies who was supposed to be tending the children of a visiting diplomat. To make matters worse, one of those children became lost for a short period of time and could have cost the hotel a fortune in lawsuits if Rachel hadn't accidentally found the five-year-old boy. He'd been wandering around in the car park below the hotel where she'd gone for her car after running from Stephen's room.

After unburdening herself to her best friend, Liz, while the initial shock and pain of his betrayal wore off, she started to realize what a pitiful excuse of a man he really was. His first reaction at seeing her in his suite had been one of anger because she'd dared to come to his room without permission. No tears, no sorrow, no apology. *So much for his repeated declarations of undying love....*

A day later he came after her, repentant, but the damage had been done. When she wouldn't listen to him, he begged Liz to reason with her. When that didn't work, he bombarded her with telephone calls and left messages on her answering machine, threatening to fire her and blame her for the other nanny's negligence if she refused to get in touch with him.

But his scare tactics no longer had the power to touch her because he'd killed any love she'd ever felt for him. Without hesitation she resigned and began making preparations to fly to Spain. Though she had hoped to save a little more money before leaving New York, at that point nothing mattered but to get away and find Brian.

Her brother was all she had left in this world and he was out there somewhere. *But never in her wildest dreams would she have imagined him being hunted by the police.*

When she thought of her darling brother, her heart ached and the heavy emptiness intensified. She tossed and turned for what seemed like hours, realizing she couldn't do anything to find him, not when the police with all their resources hadn't come up with any news.

Probably the best thing was to go back to New York and pray that Brian would call or write her a letter soon. Maybe he'd tried to contact her while she'd been gone!

Now that she'd paid Señor de Riano, she couldn't afford this expensive hotel another night. In fact it didn't make sense to remain in Spain another day, especially when she needed to look for a new job. Since she had no reason to see the *señor* again, there was nothing to prevent her from leaving.

But even as she reasoned that way, his forceful image filled her thoughts. She tried to imagine his face without any shadows lurking in the depths of his fiery eyes. Since meeting him, her heartbeat had accelerated to a frenzied rhythm, and now it prevented her falling asleep. She had no idea when oblivion finally took over.

A tap on the door followed by a maid's voice aroused Rachel from a disorienting sleep. She lifted her groggy head from the bed, grimacing at the sight of her wrinkled skirt and blouse. She'd never slept in her clothes before. "It is nine o'clock, Señorita Ellis," she said in heavily accented English. "You wish breakfast now?"

Rachel couldn't believe she'd slept so long. She scrambled off the bed and hurried toward the bathroom, thanking the maid and asking her to leave the tray on the table at the other end of the spacious room.

Checkout was in an hour. That would barely give her time to get ready and make plane reservations. Since washing and blow-drying her hair would take too long, she hurried in and out of the shower, then spent the next few minutes brushing the silvery blond strands and drawing the hair back from her face in a twist where her mother's pearl earrings would be seen to advantage.

She'd anticipated her first meeting with Brian taking place at the monastery and she'd purchased a short-sleeved, tailored white dress with navy piping in a summery cotton. She knotted the navy rope belt around her slender waist and slipped into white Italian leather sandals. It had been important that Brian be proud of her.

Poor Brian. The mere thought of his tragic dilemma produced a shiver and left her with a nervous stomach that rebelled at the thought of food. But last evening's incident—which precipitated her ending up in Señor de Riano's strong arms—taught her she'd better not go anywhere without a meal.

Disgusted with herself because she couldn't seem to stop thinking about him, she moved across the room and forced herself to eat one of the hot buttered rolls. A juicy peach had been sliced and was sweet to the taste. The kitchen had provided strong hot coffee, which was a pleasant surprise, and she wondered if that were standard fare for American tourists.

While she drank the steaming sweet liquid, she picked up the phone and rang through to the concierge to see about getting an early afternoon flight back to New York. Within a few minutes she'd made arrangements to be on the one leaving at twelve. At that point she prevailed on the telephonist to put through a call to police headquarters in Seville where she gave them the details of her departure time and flight number.

With that accomplished, she reasoned that if she returned her rental car to the airport an hour before her flight, she would still have an hour to sightsee.

Though her heart wasn't in it, she couldn't sit around here any longer. In fact, she preferred to be gone from this place so there could be no possibility of another confrontation with Señor de Riano. The dark landowner's righteous indignation could be rather terrifying, and she had no wish to repeat yesterday's experience.

Besides, if the *señor* were right and Brian was still in the area, there was the remote chance she might spot her brother.

Oh, who was she kidding?

Tears burned her eyes. She hadn't seen him for six years. Perhaps his character had changed beyond recognition and he was as guilty as the Swede. The *señor* was well within his rights to think her a naive little fool.

Another shudder rippled through her body and she put the empty cup back on the tray, ready to tackle her luggage. She'd only brought one suitcase and a hand carryall for her toiletries. It didn't take much time to finish packing her things and walk through the corridor to reception so she could check out and pay the bill.

A pretty girl at the desk flashed her a pleasant smile. "Señor de Riano has already taken care of it and has instructed me to tell you that you may stay here as long as you wish."

Rachel had to clamp down hard on her emotions. She was convinced his largesse was motivated by something other than generosity. Familiar stirrings of anger welled up all over again. "Be that as it may, I'm leaving now and would like my passport please."

"Of course." If the other girl was surprised, she didn't let it show.

Rachel put the passport in her handbag, picked up her bags and marched out the doors into a wall of crushing heat. She wondered if she would ever get used to it, then scoffed at the notion since she'd be back in New York by evening.

As she drove away from the Alcazar, she speculated on the *señor*'s reasons for paying for her room. He owed her nothing and was intentionally trying to make her feel guilty. Why? To underline the fact that Brian had affected the *señor* in profound ways he had only alluded to?

Within forty-five minutes Rachel's car skirted Seville's whitewashed houses and baroque facades which overflowed with bougainvillea. After consulting her street map, she turned onto the Paseo de las Delicias and headed for the Giralda tower, but the morning traffic had become a nightmare. She was forced to slow her pace and to keep looking in her rearview mirror because the man behind her continued to press on his horn.

That's when she noticed a sleek, metallic blue Astin Martin Lagonda several cars behind that seemed to turn everywhere she did. At first she wasn't overly concerned. Then a truck practically ran her off the road, forcing her to turn down the first alley she came to, and her heart skipped a beat when the blue car stayed right with her.

She wished she could see who was driving, but the bright sun shining on the tinted glass made it impossible. Without wasting another second, she pulled into the first available space along the side of the narrow street, hoping the other car would drive by and disappear. But the blue car also found a free spot several vehicles ahead, signaling that this was no coincidence.

Could it possibly be Brian driving that sinfully expensive sports car? Had he found out she'd been inquiring about him yesterday and was trying to make contact?

She got out of her car and locked it, waiting to see what the driver of the other car would do. At the sight of Señor de Riano stepping out from behind the wheel and striding purposefully toward her, that fleeting sense of apprehension and anticipation quickly changed to fury.

If he'd had a legitimate reason for wanting to talk to her, he could have approached her in the foyer of the hotel while she was checking out. Instead, he'd been watching her every move and had followed her all the way from Carmona, no doubt hoping she'd lead him to Brian. As far as she was concerned, he'd thrown down the gauntlet, which entitled her to do exactly the same!

But he didn't fight fairly. There were no work pants and shirtsleeves today. Her breath caught involuntarily as her gaze took in the immaculate sand-colored linen suit molding his tall, powerful body, proclaiming him the wealthy, sophisticated Sevillian.

Only the black hair spilling over his forehead hinted at the primitive side of his nature. But she knew it existed and she had already been the recipient of that eruptive force. She didn't understand *it* or the chemistry that drew her to him in spite of the enmity between them, and the closer he came, the more she instinctively shied away.

"Why tip your hand so soon, *señor?*" she scorned her adversary in retaliation, alarmed by the possessive glint in those black eyes wandering over her face and body as if she were the prize he'd come to collect after winning the battle. "Another half hour and I might have led you straight to Brian!"

CHAPTER THREE

"YESTERDAY your appearance in the village set tongues wagging from Jabugo to Seville. On the outside chance that your brother got wind of it and was lured from his hiding place, the police and I were hoping he might have followed *you* into town this morning."

His explanation—which if he were telling the truth could be corroborated by the police—made a strange kind of sense since she'd been hoping the same thing. But she hadn't expected to meet up with Señor de Riano again. His presence threw her into a state of panic and confusion which had little to do with her brother.

She unconsciously smoothed moist palms over her hips, a nervous gesture his keen eyes followed with disarming intensity.

"My disappointment is greater than yours that Brian didn't step out of the car instead of you." *Which wasn't altogether true, but she'd rather lie than admit that to him.*

After an uncomfortable silence he said, "To be frank, *señorita,* all thoughts of catching sight of your brother went out of my head when I saw that *idiota* run you off the road. No doubt the police have cited him by now, but it is a credit to your driving skill that I did not have to call an ambulance to take you to hospital.''

His compliment came as a surprise, but he never said or did anything without a motive, and she absolutely refused to be manipulated by him.

"As you can see, I'm fine, and my brother is nowhere in sight. I never asked to be in your debt, *señor,*" she blurted out vehemently. "I would pay you back for the hotel room, but for a reason known only to yourself, you wish to keep me beholden to you." She spoke boldly, noticing the way his dark brows furrowed in displeasure. "I think you enjoy watching me squirm. If I need protection while I'm here in Spain, it's from you, *señor,* no one else."

"¡Madre de Dios!" he stormed in his native tongue, seemingly more angry than he'd been yesterday. It made her happy that she'd managed to get under his skin; however, she didn't like the fact that they'd become the center of attention on a street swarming with tourists milling in and out of the bars and souvenir shops.

"I'm afraid you'll have to excuse me. I'm on my way to the airport."

"Not quite yet." In the next instant he grasped her wrist, and hauled her against him, preventing further movement. For a brief moment she was unbearably aware of his thigh brushing hers, and the heat of his hand on her flesh. "There's an urgent matter I need to discuss with you," he muttered in a peremptory tone.

"I—I don't think so, *señor.*" His nearness was proving a threat to her peace of mind which she didn't dare analyze too closely.

"Not even if it has a direct bearing on your brother?"

"Does this mean that I'm going to hear about his *other* sins?" she returned swiftly.

His grip tightened. "It is up to you if we converse here, in front of hundreds of strangers. I'd prefer to take you to my home where we'll be assured of privacy."

He wanted to take her to his villa? Her pulse raced. "You live too far away. I'll miss my flight."

He flicked her a dark, unreadable glance. "You mean your brother didn't tell you I have a house in Seville as well as the mountains?"

Anger over his continual erroneous assumptions brought a rush of heat to her cheeks. "I only know enough about you to be sorry I ever trespassed on your property."

"If you recall, I told you to go back to the States on the next available flight," he reminded her with a hauteur that made her want to slap his face. "But you didn't heed my advice."

"So that makes me suspect in your eyes and now I'm your prisoner. Is that it?" she cried out in frustration.

"If that's what you want to believe, then I won't attempt to persuade you differently."

She tried to hold herself apart from him. "You said yourself that the police haven't caught Brian, and we know he hasn't given himself up. I don't understand the need for a talk.''

"You will." His voice had an ominous ring. Without giving her a choice, he forced her to accompany him to his car where he told her in no uncertain terms to get in.

Once her door was shut, he went around and levered himself in the driver's seat with a fluid motion, filling the rich leather interior with his vital presence.

They might be enemies, but she had no defense against the insidious invasion of his sensual appeal. She didn't want to be this aware of his hard body, of the scent of the soap he used.

"Wh-what about my car? It needs to be returned to the rental agency."

"Someone on my staff will take care of it as soon as we get to the house."

While he turned on the powerful engine and edged into traffic, she glanced at her watch, trying not to notice the play of muscle across his back and shoulders as he shifted gears. "There isn't much time before I have to check in at the airport, *señor.*"

"You can always take another flight," he replied in a matter-of-fact tone, relegating her concerns to so much trivia. For the time being, he had her at his mercy.

He drove his car expertly, maneuvering through the traffic with a speed that took her breath, yet oddly enough she felt safe and taken care of, the exact same feelings she'd experienced in his arms yesterday.

They left the main autoroute to travel through the center of the city. The *señor* remained unsettlingly quiet and eventually they reached a beautiful residential area of seventeenth-century houses off the Calle Susana.

If she'd come to Spain for a holiday, nothing would have prevented her from exploring the twisting alleyways. Every turn revealed charming white houses with ochre-framed windows and a profusion of geraniums and petunias spilling over patios and grillwork to enchant the eye.

But the fact that Brian was in so much trouble made it impossible for her to enjoy this totally unexpected insight into the privileged life of a native Andalusian. It was almost as if he'd brought her here deliberately, so she could experience the contrast between the blessed and the damned and writhe a little more.

When they pulled up in front of what could only be described as a small, exquisite mansion, Rachel knew real fear. Obviously Señor Vincente came from a monied background that traced its origins to the Spanish aristocracy.

What paltry sum she could afford to pay a solicitor to defend Brian would be laughable compared to the army of legal counsel already in his employ who'd quash any attempts she might make to prove his innocence. She had no delusions on that score and she refused to meet his questioning glance after he got out of the car and came around to help her.

"I've asked Sharom to prepare us a meal which I think we'll eat indoors today, since the heat still seems to be having its effect on you."

Her eyes flashed purple, as much from anger as from the sensations she experienced whenever he got too close to her and touched her as he was doing now, guiding her to the entrance with his hand almost intimately curved at the juncture of her waist and hip.

Rachel held herself rigid in the hope he wouldn't know how his proximity affected her. "It's not the heat but your autocratic, unjust assumptions about my brother's supposedly vile character that are upsetting me, *señor*."

She thought he was going to open the doors beneath an overhang of bougainvillea and didn't understand when he unexpectedly grasped her chin, lifting her flushed face to his relentless scrutiny. "You can still defend him when you've known next to nothing about his activities over the last six years?"

She was sharply conscious of the heavily perfumed air and his warm breath teasing her lips. A tiny nerve throbbed at the corner of his hard mouth, diverting her attention. She forgot what he'd asked her.

Without conscious thought she lifted dazed eyes to him, searching the black depths of his, her body so alive to his exciting male aura and the palpable tension hovering between them, she could scarcely breathe.

"*¡Dios!*" His husky murmur penetrated to her bones. In that unrehearsed protest of naked emotion she heard many things and wondered with pounding heart if she might be disturbing him as profoundly.

"Tío Vincente?"

At the sound of a woman's voice, Rachel immediately jerked away from him, breaking the strange intimacy they'd shared. A black-haired, voluptuous beauty no more than twenty, twenty-one, stood in the doorway, wearing a stunning black-and-white dress that looked Italian in design. Her dark, serious eyes stared in undisguised puzzlement at Rachel.

"Ayee—" she cried out softly, her slender, manicured hands covering her mouth in unfeigned shock.

"Carmen— You forget your manners," the *señor* quipped, clearly not pleased by the interruption.

"Pero—"

"Speak English in front our guest, *por favor,"* he demanded, and ushered a reluctant but curious Rachel inside the marble foyer.

Was Carmen the *señor's wife?* she agonized. It wasn't uncommon for a man in his thirties to take a young bride, especially in wealthy families who safeguarded their pedigrees through arranged marriages planned from birth.

"Señorita Ellis, meet my niece, Carmen, who lives with me."

The explanation of their relationship shouldn't have mattered to Rachel. But to her alarm, she found that it did. Very much, in fact.

"How do you do, Carmen?" Rachel would have extended her hand but held back when the younger woman's beautiful, haunted black eyes filled with tears.

"You are Rach—"

"*Sí,* Carmen," the *señor* broke in grimly, before his niece could finish. "Señorita Ellis is Brian Ellis's sister. The resemblance is uncanny. ¿*Verdad?*"

Carmen's countenance changed and she flicked angry eyes to her uncle. "You said he was a liar. But he wasn't lying about *her!*"

"Enough, *chica,*" her uncle warned.

"Why do you continue to believe the worst about him?" Her passionate cry reverberated in the richly paneled foyer.

The slash of one dark brow dipped ominously. "We will talk later, Carmen."

"You mean *you* will do the talking and I will listen. It has always been that way. I think I hate you." The bitterness of her pronouncement lingered as she ran across the elegant foyer and up the marble staircase.

Rachel stared after her, realizing that Brian was at the bottom of their contretemps, otherwise why would Carmen have chosen this moment to erupt in front of Rachel—in English no less—and embarrass her uncle?

"You'll have to forgive my niece," he said with surprising calm. "She hasn't been herself lately. Now—" His watchful gaze captured hers for a breathless moment. "Give me the key to your car and I'll instruct Felipe to return it to the rental agency."

In the heat of the moment she'd forgotten all about the car. With less than steady fingers she opened her handbag and searched for it.

"Here." She dropped it in his palm, making sure there was no contact.

His mouth twitched, letting her know he found her action amusing. "You are welcome to use the guest bath at the end of the hall behind the stairs. When you're ready, we'll have lunch in the dining room off the *sala* to your right."

"I don't need to freshen up, *señor,* and I'm not hungry." She was sick to death of his civility which cloaked an underlying motive for bringing her here. "After witnessing Carmen's reaction, I can tell she's painfully in love with my brother.

"Which was the greater crime in your eyes? Stealing from you, or falling in love with your niece?" she taunted. "It doesn't take a genius to figure out that you don't approve."

His eyes narrowed. "For reasons I don't wish to divulge just yet, I prefer this conversation to take place in my study. *Por favor.*"

He indicated she accompany him through the mirrored sitting room with its heavy black and gilt furniture. It lead to another room with dark wood paneling, walls of books, ornately framed portraits, and a fireplace. The leather furniture and heavy Moorish lamps proclaimed it a man's room, sumptuous enough for nobility.

He shut the double paneled doors, entombing them, at least that was what it felt like to Rachel. "Sit down, Miss Ellis."

While he poured himself a drink from the sideboard, she took a chair near the huge wood-carved desk. "Would you care for a sherry from the finest bodega in Jerez?" he called over his shoulder, "or do you wish to forego all the amenities and plunge straight for the bull?'' His reference to her remark about the cruelty of the Spanish *corrida* did not escape her.

"Bait me all you want, *señor*. You are bigger and stronger than I am, and you're holding me against my will. My brother really got to you, didn't he?'' she goaded, not caring what she said because his arrogance and insufferable male pride made her so angry.

"*¡Por Dios!*'' he exploded, and drank the amber liquid in one gulp. "Next I suppose that fertile imagination of yours expects me to throw you down on the cold marble floor and ravish your slender white body without pity.''

"No,'' she answered primly though her bloodstream surged in fear and excitement because she could arouse his emotions so easily, *and* worse, because the sensual picture he'd just painted had flashed through her mind seconds before he'd put words to the thought.

"The great Vincente de Riano would never degrade himself with the sister of a criminal as loathsome as Brian Ellis. I am safe, *señor,* I have no doubt of it.''

He muttered something else undecipherable beneath his breath and brought his empty sherry glass down so hard on the sideboard she heard it crack. The sound pleased her though she felt her limbs quaking.

He slowly turned around and faced her, his expression grim, his hard-muscled physique tall and imposing. How had she dared speak to him like that? She didn't know what had come over her.

"Contrary to your personal opinion of me, I am not a man without some sensibilities and you've proven to me that your love for your brother is real." He actually sounded sincere, which threw her off base even more because she didn't know what to believe where he was concerned. One minute he maddened her, the next minute he... he...

"Your tenacity in endeavoring to find him, and your devotion to him in spite of his crime, however misguided, is not only admirable, but rare."

By this time he had taken a seat behind his desk, studying her through veiled eyes. Though his words should have thawed some of the ice around her heart, she was suddenly more nervous than before because he reminded her of a jungle cat who appeared to be slumbering contentedly, but in reality was ready to pounce at any moment.

"The woman I've seen in action does not act or sound like the same woman who was fired from her job at the Kennedy Plaza less than two weeks ago for carelessly losing the child of an important Arab diplomat, thereby putting his young life in jeopardy."

Rachel blinked. *Stephen truly did have a cruel streak.* Somehow it didn't surprise her that he'd made good his threat, hoping to ruin her chances for a job with Señor de Riano.

His dark brows furrowed speculatively. "You don't deny it?"

Maybe it was her imagination but for a fleeting moment, Rachel thought she glimpsed a flash of disappointment in his eyes; however, it was gone as fast as it came and she couldn't be sure of anything.

"If I told you I was falsely accused, you wouldn't believe me any more than you believed Brian," she said in a brittle tone. "There's no point in defending myself."

"First my niece, now you." His lips quirked, displaying the first sign of levity since they'd met. It transformed his features. When he looked like that, her heart turned over and she could wish she were in Spain for an entirely different reason.

A tap on the door jerked Rachel from her traitorous thoughts. One of the *señor*'s staff quietly entered the room and the two of them conversed in unintelligible Spanish. She watched her car key change hands before the older man gave his employer a brief nod and left to carry out his instructions.

When the *señor* turned to her, an expressionless mask had slipped back in place, making her doubt what she thought she'd glimpsed moments earlier.

"I called your hotel to obtain a background check on you. The man in charge painted a picture that does not fit my gut assessment. I'm still waiting for an explanation."

"*Why?*" she retorted. "In your eyes I'm already as guilty as my brother."

He sat forward, his fiery gaze focused on her. "I'm prepared to be convinced otherwise because the man was too ready with his character assassination, too emotional in his delivery, leading me to deduce that the two of you have had a relationship outside your work, that perhaps you're in the middle of a lovers' quarrel."

The *señor* saw and understood too much. Rachel couldn't sustain his piercing glance and looked away.

"I thought so," he murmured in a low, controlled voice. "So, are you going to destroy my tentative belief in you and allow me to assume that were you negligent in your duties toward the little boy in your charge, that I should find someone else to be a temporary nanny to my little Luisa?"

Luisa—

Rachel's hands curved around the arms of the chair in a death grip. Vincente de Riano had a child? *That meant he had a wife.* The news was devastating.

"*¿Señorita?*" he prompted, unaware of her turmoil.

"Wh-where is her mother?" she stammered when she could finally get the words out.

Lines darkened his face, adding to its brooding quality. "Physically she has recovered from a difficult delivery which required a Cesarean section. Emotionally, she is not well...." His voice trailed, sounding far away. "Both she and the baby are fortunate to be alive."

Her head came up abruptly. *"Baby?"*

"She's seven weeks old today," he murmured.

His daughter was practically a newborn. Rachel stirred restlessly because the problem involving Brian would of necessity have added to the *señor*'s distress at a time when his wife needed him most. Rachel didn't know how to deal with the weight around her heart. She tried looking anywhere except at him.

"The doctor examined her yesterday and suggested a vacation is in order. Hopefully a change of scene away from the responsibility of caring for Luisa should do her some good."

A bitter laugh escaped her lips. "And you're asking *me,* one of the infamous *Ellis* clan who was fired from her job as a nanny, to watch after *your* own flesh and blood?"

Furious with herself for having gotten emotionally involved, she jumped to her feet, unable to remain seated. "If this is the urgent matter you wished to discuss with me, then your sense of humor is as twisted as your sense of honor."

She wasn't normally this volatile, but her growing attraction to the *señor* after only twenty-four hours in his company made the idea of remaining under his roof while his wife was away not only dangerous, but unthinkable.

"Indeed." His black eyes flashed a warning, but she was past caring.

"You've wasted your time, Señor Riano, and you've caused me to miss my plane. But never fear, as you succinctly pointed out to me yesterday, there are half a dozen flights leaving daily. I'll take a taxi to the airport and wait for another one. You can ship my belongings to my New York apartment. I'll make up the difference with the next installment!"

He moved so fast, he met her at the double doors and she careered into him. His hands shot out to steady her, sending another thrill of alarm through her body. Desire for him engulfed her and she tore herself away, but it was too late. The damage had been done, and the imprint of his solid chest and thighs would remain to torture her.

Shame so consumed her that she was finding it impossible to fight her feelings for him when she knew he belonged to someone else.

"Wouldn't you like to see Luisa before you turn down my offer?" His deep voice seemed to permeate to her very fingertips. "Or am I underestimating the strength of your feelings for the man you left behind, that you are already regretting your precipitous flight?"

Her head reared back. "Whatever he told you, he would be lying. There is no man in my life." The study rang with her firm declaration.

The *señor* examined her taut features as if weighing the veracity of her words. With a sudden negligent shrug of his shoulders he said, "Then I don't see the problem. You've admitted that you have no job to return to, that your funds are dangerously low. I'm offering you a generous salary, plus living accommodations which will allow you to be waited on while you give Luisa the love and attention she needs during her mother's absence."

He moved closer. "It will buy you another week." His eyes glittered. "Perhaps in that amount of time your brother will have been found, and you can have your long-awaited reunion with him."

She shook her head, in awe of his cunning. "You almost persuade me, *señor,* but my chances of hearing from my brother will be much greater if I return to New

York, and *you* know it." Her gaze defied him. "What is it you *really* want?"

She probably imagined the brief flare of admiration in his dark eyes because a calculating smile broke the corner of his mouth, a mouth she tried desperately hard not to look at or think about.

Without saying anything, he strode back to his desk and spoke to someone on the intercom, his gaze never wavering from Rachel's taut features. A female voice answered and another undecipherable conversation ensued. It ended with the woman saying, *"Sí, señor."* Those were two words Rachel understood well enough. Whoever was at the other end had promised to do his bidding.

He lounged with effortless grace against the desk, his powerful legs crossed at the ankles, drawing her attention to his superb male physique. She resented his charisma which went much deeper than sheer physical appeal. She didn't want to be attracted to him, didn't invite it.

"Would you care for a drink while we wait, Miss Ellis? Perhaps *now* you're in need of one."

"I rather think it's the other way around, that perhaps it is *you* who is in need of sustenance. Feel free to indulge yourself again, *señor,*" she mocked to counteract the primitive emotions he aroused. "After all, you are the king of the castle, as your niece said," she added unwisely.

"¡Por Dios!"

On the heels of his explosion she heard a baby cry. Suddenly a dark-haired, middle-aged woman came through the doors and swept past Rachel, carrying a fluffy white bundle in her arms.

Rachel watched in fascination as Señor de Riano thanked the woman, then took the baby and rested her body against his broad shoulder. Obviously no stranger to his daughter, he smoothed her tiny back beneath the baby blanket with his large, tanned hand and crooned softly to her.

Though the words might be foreign, Rachel understood their universal message for he spoke with incredible tenderness, bringing a lump to her throat.

Unbidden, her mind flicked back to various moments in the past when Stephen had come to find Rachel while she was on duty tending a lively toddler or a sweet little baby. Never once had he stopped to play with them or hold them.

She should have picked up on that illuminating clue. He had no real affection for anyone but himself, and until that changed, he would never make a good parent. Certainly he would never have cuddled one of her charges as the *señor* was doing now, oblivious of soiling his elegant linen suit.

Like two sides of a coin, Vincente de Riano presented one face to his enemies, another to those he loved. *What would it feel like to be the recipient of that love?*

The baby knew because she immediately stopped crying and made a gurgling sound which produced a low, attractive chuckle from her father. The older woman beamed in delight before dropping a curtsey to both her employer and Rachel on her way out of the room.

His proud glance darted to Rachel. "One day, Luisa is going to break many hearts."

Rachel didn't doubt it. Not if she resembled her father who was the most disturbingly attractive male she'd ever met in her life.

"In all probability, she will follow in your footsteps," he added the aside so quietly, it took a moment before Rachel understood his meaning, and a prickly sensation broke out over her skin. But if he was referring to Stephen, he was way off the mark. Stephen was too egotistical to allow his heart to be broken.

Her host's black eyes trapped hers. "Wouldn't you at least like one look at the *niña* before you go?" Then he started toward her. "Or are you afraid she will tug too strongly at your heart and prevent you from leaving as soon as you're determined to do."

Rachel's heart was already pounding out of control. *It's not the baby I'm afraid of.*

She wanted to run and keep on running, but an unseen force kept her in place while he lowered the baby from his shoulder and removed the edges of the blanket. Rachel couldn't refrain from taking a peek.

To her shock, hair as pale as moonlight capped the angelic little face that stared up at her, resembling someone very dear. Someone who meant more to Rachel than anyone else in the world.

"I don't believe it."

Señor de Riano eyed her intently. "Except for inheriting Carmen's black eyes and olive skin, Luisa would probably be your mirror image at the same age."

"It's like looking at all the old baby photos mother took of Brian and me," she whispered in absolute awe, and reached for Luisa, holding her warm little body against her shoulder.

"Luisa is *Brian's* daughter, not yours," she marveled aloud, experiencing a strange, exhilarating elation that was all out of proportion to the gravity of the situation.

A perplexed expression broke out on his intelligent face. "You thought *I* was the baby's father?"

"Yes. Y-you said, *my* Luisa." In giddy reaction, she kissed the downy head, inhaling the sweet smell of baby powder.

"She might as well be." His voice conveyed a possessive ring. "My pregnant wife died in the same light plane crash that killed Carmen's parents three years ago."

Dear God.

"I've looked after my niece ever since. Though she made the most serious mistake of her young life getting involved with your brother, Luisa is innocent and deserves everything I'm capable of giving her."

Rachel didn't doubt the sincerity of his statement. She'd seen him interact with the baby and knew that his affection for her was genuine, that she'd flourish under his love.

In fact Rachel admired him immensely for taking on such a vital responsibility and was grateful for his devotion to her new little niece who would want for nothing living beneath the *señor*'s roof.

But the fact still remained that Brian was Luisa's father. *He* should be the one taking care of Carmen and his child. Time was passing that he could never get back, and his debt to the *señor* was growing. *Where was he?* she agonized.

"Does Brian know about Luisa?"

"Carmen was five months' pregnant when he disappeared, but she didn't tell me about her condition until she could no longer hide the evidence. It's possible that your brother knew he was going to be a father long before he abandoned Carmen to her fate."

Abandoned. Rachel flinched from the word and refused to believe it. "What does Carmen say?"

He rubbed the back of his neck absently. "I'm afraid my niece hasn't been too communicative of late."

Having witnessed Carmen's heated anger for herself, Rachel didn't doubt his words. "But it's also possible that Carmen either didn't have a chance to tell Brian the truth, or chose not to tell him the truth, before he went away."

He gave a careless shrug. "What difference does it make, *señorita?* The end result is the same. He is gone."

"If he didn't know he was going to be a father, then it makes all the difference in the world!" she snapped at him. To her chagrin Luisa started to cry, but Rachel was too strung up to stop talking. "Our father deserted us in our adolescence and it practically destroyed Brian. Do you honestly think he would repeat history if he knew he had a daughter who needed him?"

The *señor's* eyes blazed ferociously. "What is it they say? Like father, like son."

"But you're not a father, and you're certainly not Luisa's father!" she flung back, trying to calm the baby by bouncing her and patting her back. "So you're in no position to judge."

He straightened to his full, intimidating height. "If your brother has disappeared for good, then I will be the one raising Luisa, and I'll formally adopt her."

Rachel's eyes widened in shock. "You can't! She's Carmen's daughter!"

"That's true. But what you don't know is that my niece was affianced before your brother ruined her life. Raimundo de Leon comes from one of the finest families in Spain and he is still willing to marry her."

"Provided Luisa isn't part of the package. Is that what you're saying?" Rachel cried out in disgust, causing the baby to protest even more vigorously than before. "Is that the kind of coldhearted man you want for your niece?" Her chest heaved, communicating her distress to the baby who by now was howling in earnest.

Raising her voice above the din Rachel said, "Surely Carmen couldn't be a party to any such bargain. It sounds like something only a despot like *you* could have engineered. My congratulations, *señor*. I didn't think I could hate you any more than I did yesterday when you ordered me off your property, but I was wrong!"

His expression turned black as thunderclouds before a storm, incensing her even more. She couldn't resist adding, "You're a throwback from the Middle Ages who doesn't belong in this century! It's a miracle Carmen hasn't run away yet. Make no mistake, I'll fight for custody of Luisa myself before I let you have a chance to ruin her life, too!"

CHAPTER FOUR

BEFORE SHE COULD countenance it, he closed the distance between them and took the crying infant from her arms. A few words of comfort and a cuddle, and Luisa went quiet. The master's touch.

His eyes flicked to Rachel's and they faced each other as adversaries.

"As I told you earlier, you rush to conclusions before you know all the facts. Raimundo would marry Carmen under any circumstances and raise Luisa as his own, defying his family's wishes."

His chastening words brought a flush to her cheeks.

"It is Carmen who persists in the mistaken belief that Brian will come back to her and she has refused Raimundo's overtures. As a result, she has focused her entire life on the baby," he countered. "Her devotion to Luisa has been nothing short of phenomenal, even at the cost to her personal health."

Rachel blinked. "Is your niece ill?"

"She had toxemia throughout her troubled pregnancy. The doctors have warned against her getting pregnant again. For this reason, she's convinced Luisa will be her only child and she has become overly protective of her." In a loving gesture, he laid his bronzed cheek alongside the baby's, bringing another lump to

Rachel's throat. Then he lifted his head and leveled his dark gaze at her.

"It's Carmen's emotional state I'm worried about. There was a time when I couldn't keep her from spending her allowance in every fashionable boutique in Seville. Now I can't persuade her to leave the baby to shop or see old friends because she doesn't trust the staff to look after Luisa properly. Her life has become abnormal and unhealthy."

After the scenario he'd painted, Rachel's heart ached for Carmen and she could only agree with the *señor*'s assessment of his niece's obsession. Upon reflection, she realized he had to be carrying a heavy weight of personal sorrow besides his many business responsibilities.

"*Señor*—if you haven't been successful in getting her to leave Luisa for any reason, what makes you think she'd let *me* tend the baby? I'm a total stranger."

An enigmatic expression crossed over his face. "That's true. However, you're a licensed nanny. More importantly, you're Luisa's aunt. If you were to convince Carmen that you love Luisa, that you would like the opportunity to get to know her before you return to the States—that it might be years before you will get back to Spain again—Carmen might be willing to entrust the baby to your care for a brief period."

Rachel rubbed her arms nervously, wondering why she was even entertaining the idea of staying when the *señor* didn't like or trust her.

"If Carmen is nursing, then it's only natural she wouldn't want to be separated from Luisa yet."

Lines darkened his face. "She had to stop nursing in the hospital because her milk gave Luisa jaundice. The baby had to be transfused before she could be brought home."

"Poor Carmen," she whispered, beginning to see the situation through the *señor*'s eyes. No matter how much Rachel wanted to excuse Brian's behavior, she could understand how Vincente de Riano would find her brother's sudden disappearance not only suspicious, but unforgivable.

For all intents and purposes, it looked as if Brian *had* abandoned Carmen and left her quite literally at death's door. What was it Rachel's mother had once said to her and Brian?

I can't forgive your father for walking out on us. Twice I passed through the valley of death to bring his babies into the world. And he wasn't even there. Do you know where he was? He was with that other woman. Think of it, children. Just think of it.

In anguish of spirit, Rachel turned away from her host, fighting to get her emotions under control. Though the pattern looked familiar and the negative evidence was stacked against him, a part of Rachel stubbornly refused to believe Brian was cut from the same cloth as her father.

But if that were true, *why had Brian been gone such a long time? Why hadn't he contacted Carmen? Or Rachel?*

Suddenly her host was talking. "Naturally I cannot force you to stay, *señorita*. Neither of us would have envisioned, let alone invited, the situation in which my niece and your brother are embroiled. I would not blame you if you chose to go back to the States before the day is out. Particularly when it is evident there is someone waiting most anxiously for you. I will drive you to the airport myself if that is what y—"

"Tío Vincente?" Carmen picked that moment to rush into the room and reach for her daughter. But instead of the *señor* relinquishing Luisa, he said something in rapid Spanish that forced Carmen to turn in Rachel's direction. A guilt-ridden expression marred her porcelainlike features.

"Excuse me for interrupting, Miss Ellis, but it's time for me to feed Luisa and put her back down for the rest of her nap."

Rachel sensed her host's piercing gaze, making her slightly breathless. *Now* was the time to announce her own plans and ask the *señor* to drive her to the airport.

But the temptation to remain another week in Spain without money worries so she could try to discover Brian's whereabouts on her own caused Rachel to say something quite different.

Turning to Carmen she said, "I—I was hoping you would let me feed her. I'm anxious to get acquainted with my new little niece. Already I love her." Her voice quivered unintentionally and, without meaning to, her glance lifted to the *señor*'s for a brief moment.

"You see—she's a part of Brian, and I love him more than anyone else in the world. There isn't anything I wouldn't do for him."

"That's right, Carmen," her host chimed in with a satisfied smile that made Rachel wish she could have recanted her words, but not at the expense of having to go home before she could search a little longer for her brother.

Señor de Riano believed he'd managed to manipulate her into doing exactly what he wanted. She kept telling herself that she had fallen in with his plans strictly for Brian's and ultimately Carmen's sake.

"Why don't you take Miss Ellis upstairs and show her the nursery? We can put off lunch for another half hour and I'll bring the baby a fresh bottle." He placed Luisa in Carmen's arms and lowered his head to kiss her fair hair once more.

For an instant, Rachel saw Carmen's expression soften, belying the younger woman's earlier assertion that she hated her uncle. It seemed the *señor* wasn't above getting the baby her formula. When he chose to exert it, apparently no woman was immune to his charm, not Carmen, and certainly not Luisa who quieted down immediately after he took her from Rachel.

But Rachel knew she had her work cut out to win Carmen's trust, enough to allow her to care for the baby in Carmen's absence. That might not be so easily accomplished, especially when Carmen appeared hesitant at the idea of Rachel accompanying her anywhere.

"Your uncle tells me you're a wonderful mother. Perhaps I could watch you give Luisa her bottle this feeding, and you could teach me what to do."

Carmen looked far from convinced. "Have you ever been around a baby before?"

"Miss Ellis is a certified nanny, *chica,*" her uncle inserted smoothly. "She tends other people's babies for a living." Which comment made Rachel feel somewhat guilty because she was no longer employed.

"But Carmen and I both know a nanny can never take the place of a mother," Rachel rushed to defend Carmen's unspoken fears before the *señor* could say anything else, causing the younger woman to eye Rachel a little less suspiciously.

"All I can do is observe you, Carmen, then try to do the right thing for Luisa, if you'll let me. I'd like your daughter to know that there's another person in the world who is related to her and loves her very much. A child needs all the love it can get," she said, her voice cracking.

Embarrassed to have become emotional, Rachel shifted her gaze and met the *señor*'s head-on. His unfathomable eyes burned with a mysterious intensity that was somehow personal. She trembled and turned away, hoping Carmen hadn't observed the byplay. To her relief, the younger woman appeared totally absorbed with her fussy daughter. In a quiet aside she finally said, "You can come with me if you wish."

Pleased to have made that much progress, Rachel followed her from the room, all the time aware of the *señor*'s laserlike glance on her retreating back.

When they reached the foyer, Rachel expelled her breath, not realizing she'd been holding it until now.

She hurried up the marble staircase after Carmen, struck once again by the opulence of her surroundings. Everywhere she looked, framed portraits of the Riano family, illuminated by ornately gilded wall sconces, stared back.

At the second floor, Carmen led her down a hallway to the right of the stairs where they passed a painting of a particularly striking, eighteenth-century aristocrat. He reminded her so much of the *señor*, she stopped to study it.

"That's Rodrigo de Riano, Tío Vincente's grandfather four generations back," Carmen commented. "You must have noticed the resemblance, too. But *Tío* is much more handsome, don't you think?"

"I'm afraid you've embarrassed our guest, *chica*," a deep, familiar voice unexpectedly spoke from behind Rachel's back, producing a betraying blush on her cheeks because the *señor* had witnessed her absorption with the man in the painting.

Quick to recover so he wouldn't guess how his presence set her heart thudding, she avoided looking at him and turned in his niece's direction.

Struggling to steady her voice, she said, "After looking at all the paintings, I find the entire Riano family attractive. Apparently Brian did, too. You're a very beautiful young woman, Carmen. I can well understand how you stole my brother's heart. I—I'm so sorry he wasn't there for you when the baby was born."

"Luisa and I both miss him," Carmen admitted with a catch in her throat, flashing her uncle a defiant glance underscored with pain.

Rachel bit her lip. "So do I. The truth is, I haven't seen my brother for six years. But a day hasn't gone by that I haven't thought of him and longed for his company. When my letter came back from the monastery unopened, I decided to fly to Spain and find him. He still doesn't know th-that our mother died this summer."

She heard Carmen's sharp intake of breath. "Your mother is dead?" Her soulful cry sounded genuine, as if the news mattered a great deal to her.

"*Sí, chica*. Their mother never recovered from a siege of pneumonia," her uncle affirmed not unkindly. His demeanor was so different from the aggressive hostility he'd exhibited the day before, Rachel could hardly credit that the same man inhabited his body. "That is why Miss Ellis is here," he continued to explain as if he were talking to a troubled child, unaware of Rachel's shock. "She hopes to find him and tell him the sad news."

Carmen stared at Rachel, as if to verify her uncle's words.

"Before Mother died, more than anything in the world she wanted to beg Brian's forgiveness."

"Forgiveness?" Carmen whispered, her expression one of haunted confusion.

This time two pairs of flashing black eyes centered on Rachel, waiting for an explanation.

"Mother was afraid her bitterness at our father's desertion spilled over into our lives, causing Brian to leave home prematurely. She needed to tell him how sorry she was for driving him away...." Rachel's voice trailed off.

Carmen averted her gaze, causing Rachel to suspect that her brother had confided his darkest secrets to her.

Encouraged by this reaction because it meant that Brian had truly loved this woman and that theirs hadn't been a superficial relationship as the *señor* seemed to think, Rachel added, "With her dying breath, Mother prayed Brian would find the happiness he's been searching for all these years."

"She made me promise I would visit him and tell him how much she loved him, but—" Rachel broke off, focusing on the intricate pattern of the parquetry flooring. "If he hasn't made contact with you since his disappearance, then her request may prove to be an impossible task after all."

With those words, Carmen buried her face in the baby's neck. Filled with remorse because their conversation had brought more pain to the other woman, Rachel unconsciously lifted her eyes to her host whose gaze seemed to be probing her very soul. No matter how hard she tried, Rachel couldn't look away.

"I think our little *niña* is hungry," he murmured at last, but she had an idea his mind was on other things that had nothing to do with the baby, and she wondered if her errant thoughts were as transparent.

"Here's her bottle." He handed it to Rachel, his fingers scorching hers where their skin touched. "I'll see the two of you in the dining room when you've put Luisa to bed." After an almost imperceptible nod, he strode down the hall in the opposite direction.

Rachel watched him go, not aware that the mention of the baby had prompted Carmen to vanish through the dark-paneled, double doors leading into one of the apartments. When she realized she'd been left behind, Rachel had to hurry to catch up, then came to an abrupt standstill upon entering the spacious suite.

All the bed coverings, canopy and draperies were made of white lace, like a bride. In a little alcove she spied baby furniture and an exquisite baby bed with its own white lace canopy and matching fabric at the windows. The contrast of the dark wood floor and highly polished furniture provided a stunning foil that made everything dreamy and romantic.

"I've never been in a more beautiful room in my life."

Carmen lowered the bars of the baby bed to change Luisa's diaper. "Tío Vincente had it decorated especially for me after my parents were killed. This used to be my grandparents' room before they died. The first thing we did was get rid of the ugly red velvet furnishings and faded tapestries."

Rachel could understand how a young, modern woman would find such an outmoded decor oppressive, and was touched once again by the *señor*'s sensitivity to his niece's pain while attempting to deal with his own. "Did you all live together?" she asked, aware of a burning curiosity to know everything about the *señor* and his family.

"No. My father was the firstborn son and inherited this house after my grandparents died. Now it is mine. Tío Vincente has his own villa which he prefers, but since the death of my parents, he spends most of his time with me. At least here, there are no reminders of his unborn son. His wife died in the plane crash that killed my parents."

"I know," Rachel said in a haunted whisper.

"He told you about Leonora?" Carmen sounded surprised as she lifted Luisa from the bed.

"Yes." *Though he hadn't mentioned her by name.* "He also said she was pregnant. That must have been a very painful time for the two of you. No wonder he dotes on Luisa."

Afraid her preoccupation with the *señor* was too obvious, Rachel felt it wise to change the subject. "I think it's tragic that my brother hasn't yet made the acquaintance of his own daughter."

"Brian didn't steal anything, and one day when he has cleared his name, he'll come back to me and Luisa. Then Tío Vincente will see he was wrong about him," she declared with a vehemence Rachel could only admire. "Why don't you sit in the upholstered chair? It is the most comfortable place to feed the baby."

"Are you sure?" Rachel asked, astonished to have made this much headway with Carmen. "Maybe Luisa won't want me to feed her. I'll be happy to stand by and watch."

"No. Please. When I first saw you with Tío Vincente, I didn't know what to think. I—I was afraid he had poisoned you against Brian. But I can tell that you really love him." There was a brief pause. "He used to tell me how close the two of you were while you growing up. He loved you, too."

"Thank you for sharing that with me," Rachel replied in a low voice, afraid she might burst into tears at any minute. Fortunately Luisa's needs took precedence over every other consideration.

When Carmen handed her the baby, she nestled comfortably in Rachel's arms and began sucking on the bottle's nipple with an eagerness that made both women chuckle in spite of their fragile emotions.

Rachel smiled down at her niece. "When I first caught sight of Luisa, it was Brian's face I saw, and I loved her at once."

Carmen's lips curved wistfully. "I know what you mean. Tío Vincente thinks I spend too much time with Luisa, but he doesn't understand how much pleasure it gives me to look at her. I have no photo of Brian for a reminder."

"You do *now*," Rachel pronounced. "Open my purse. Inside you'll find a wallet with a packet of pictures. You can have them. There are hundreds more where those came from."

Scarcely had she made her offer than Carmen reached for the handbag and found the treasured mementos. Except for the noisy sounds Luisa made as she drank her formula, requiring an occasional burp, the silence lengthened in the room.

Out of the corner of her eye, Rachel watched the lovely woman seated on the side of the double bed devour the various poses of Brian taken mostly in his teens before he left home. Some of them included his friends, others depicted him with Rachel and their mother.

Long after Luisa had drained her bottle and had fallen asleep in Rachel's arms, Carmen stayed planted on the bed, studying each picture over and over again. Only a woman who loved a man with all her heart and soul would care about some old photographs that probably bore little resemblance to the adult he'd become in Rachel's absence.

The more she pondered it, the more Rachel wondered how Brian could have left Carmen and just disappeared into thin air, especially if he knew a baby was on the way. Didn't he realize that the love of such a beautiful, high-class woman who had brought their daughter into the world, was his greatest blessing? Didn't he feel any responsibility toward the *señor* who had hired him solely as a favor to the good abbot whose recommendation he trusted?

She nestled Luisa against her shoulder trying to imagine Vincente de Riano acting in such a selfish, irresponsible manner, and couldn't.

Though she took exception to the authoritative way he treated her, she couldn't bring herself to stay angry with him all the time. Not after observing the protective love and tenderness he showered on Carmen and the baby.

In fact, she couldn't conceive of the *señor* being intentionally cruel to anyone, certainly not without just cause. Yesterday she'd come upon him at his villa, unannounced. Knowing what she knew now, she could see why he had assumed the worst where she was concerned. Yet despite his suspicions, he was still allowing her to stay on in his home and care for Luisa.

Once more Rachel marveled at the astounding difference between a vindictive, immature person like Stephen, and a man like Vincente de Riano....

The *señor* had every reason to feel contempt for anything and anyone connected to Brian. She could understand why in the first few minutes of meeting her, he'd demanded that she go back to the States.

And yet, in the end, he hadn't let her go.... He'd shown concern over her physical weakness, and he'd been moved by her love for her brother, enough to realize that Rachel had accrued eighteen years of positive memories of Brian on which to base her belief in his integrity, enough to offer her temporary employment while they waited for news about Brian.

"With her eyes closed, Luisa could easily be your child, *señorita*." His low, sensuous voice brought Rachel back to the present with a guilty start. "She's content enough. What she doesn't know is that it's long past time for *your* feeding, and if we don't do something about that right away, I may end up having to carry you to your bed, as well."

On that warm, teasing note, the *señor* took the baby from her arms and put Luisa in the crib without waking her.

Rachel, on the other hand, was so disturbed by his unexpected nearness and the words he murmured in her ear that when she sprang to her feet, her legs almost buckled beneath her.

Since meeting him, he was like an obsession, always on her mind. She couldn't remember a time when he didn't fill her thoughts, and that pertinent fact really frightened her, especially when she'd only known him since yesterday!

CHAPTER FIVE

So DEEP WAS HER REVERIE, Rachel hadn't even heard the *señor* enter the apartment. Neither had Carmen who, when she saw him, suddenly scrambled off the bed and started gathering up the photographs. But not before he'd plucked one from the pile for his own perusal, unnerving Rachel.

When he slipped it inside his suit jacket, Carmen flashed her a signal of distress, reading her tortured thoughts with perfect clarity.

Now the police would have a photograph of Brian to assist them in their search.

In a few swift strides, the *señor* reached the entry and opened the doors, waiting for them to exit the room with him. Careful to make no noise for fear of waking the baby, Carmen put the pictures she wanted in the drawer of an exquisite rosewood escritoire, depositing the rest in Rachel's purse.

For an infinitesimal moment, another conspiratorial look passed between her and Rachel, sealing the bond which had been forming. As Rachel passed in front of the *señor* who wore a patronizing expression on his darkly handsome face, she lifted her chin a little higher and noted out of the periphery that Carmen's jaw was set with a hardness to equal Rachel's.

The younger woman's beauty masked a strength of character and will reminiscent of her uncle's. Carmen was a de Riano after all...

Rachel followed the younger woman down the stairs to the elegant dining room, all the while cognizant of the *señor*'s disturbing interest. She could imagine that there'd been many fiery clashes between him and his niece since he'd become her guardian. She also sensed an underlying love.

Rachel's sadness intensified when she thought about Brian's entry into their lives. He'd changed the very tenor of their existence, creating pain and havoc, creating an innocent baby who needed the love of both parents.

Images of the *señor*'s suntanned face nuzzling Luisa's cheek out of love suddenly flashed into Rachel's mind. For an insane moment she wished Luisa were their baby, hers and the *señor*'s. She found herself wondering what it would be like to live with him all the time, to lie in his powerful arms throughout the long, warm Andalusian nights and experience raptu—

"Señorita Ellis?"

Crimson stained her cheeks. "Y-yes?" she stammered, aware of Carmen's curious stare, and shocked to discover the *señor* was holding out a chair so she could be seated.

How long had he been standing there scrutinizing her while she entertained some very personal and private fantasies of him which had no basis in reality?

Averting her eyes she murmured, "Thank you," and subsided into one of the rococo-styled chairs upholstered in silk damask with an Oriental motif. They surrounded the elaborately carved table which could have served for a mirror because the polished wood surface was so highly glossed.

On the wall behind Carmen stood an exquisite chest with an inlaid ivory marquetry. Rachel found it as fascinating as she did everything else in the fabulous Riano mansion which served as a veritable museum in its own right.

After seating himself at the end of the table with Rachel and Carmen at either side, the *señor* followed Rachel's gaze. "You are looking at a vargueno cabinet in the Mudejar style of the Moors. It's the only piece in the house I'm attached to."

"It's beautiful."

"Then you should see *Tío's* villa," Carmen exclaimed. "It sits on top of a mountain and I feel like a princess in a sultan's palace, looking out over the world."

"Miss Ellis did see it, briefly, at least the back patio," he said, preempting Rachel, whose face once more suffused with heat. Though the villa was magnificent, the only thing she remembered vividly was how it had felt to be held so close to his incredibly strong body as he'd carried her inert frame out of the heat to the lounger beneath the portico.

Carmen paused before taking a spoonful of the chilled fruit soup placed in front of them by one of the maids. Her black eyes, frankly curious, darted from her uncle to Rachel. "I didn't know you'd been to Aracena."

"Yes," Rachel murmured after testing the pear compote and finding it delicious. "The abbot at the monastery near Rabida told me your uncle would help me find Brian."

Lines darkened Carmen's face, making her appear older. "Instead, you found Tío Vincente."

"Which was a good thing since she was on the verge of a faint," he remarked in a conversational tone, pouring a rich red wine into each of their glasses. "Fortunately I was there to help restore her."

To her chagrin, Rachel suffered another attack of heat stroke which owed nothing to the pleasant temperature inside the room, and everything to the *señor*'s comment about an incident she'd give anything to forget, but couldn't.

"Were you ill?" Carmen sounded genuinely alarmed.

Rachel shook her head. "No, just a little dehydrated."

"And hungry," the *señor* added, not willing to leave the subject alone. "Which is why I've instructed Sharom to prepare brochette of lamb in the special way only she can do. It will melt in your mouth, as you Americans are fond of saying."

Rachel refused to look at him and instead focused her glance on Carmen who sipped at her wine and continued to study the two of them with ill-concealed interest.

"Lamb is his favorite," she confided to Rachel as if he weren't there. "*Tío* would have it for every meal. It's a good thing he can't boss Sharom around. She is the only person I know who is not intimidated by him.''

Which was saying a lot, as Rachel knew too well from personal experience; however, the arrival of the main course spared her from having to make an answering remark.

True to the *señor*'s words, the lamb and asparagus tasted like ambrosia and Rachel savored every mouthful, enjoying a second helping of crusty rolls and drinking all of her wine whose fruity taste appealed to her very much.

But when the *señor* would have refilled her glass, she put her hand over the top. Too much of that and she'd need a nap after lunch. More importantly, her instincts warned her she must stay in command and alert around her enigmatic host. Alcohol tended to lower the barriers and right now his sensual appeal went to her head far more swiftly than the most potent wine.

The glint in his eyes told her he was perfectly aware of why she had refused a second glass. Seemingly pleased, he wiped the edge of his mouth with a snowy white napkin and sat back in the chair, then centered his gaze on his niece.

"*Chica,*" he began. "Before we have dessert, I've an announcement to make."

Rachel noticed that the younger woman's face lost what little animation it had, and that she stiffened in her chair.

"The doctor tells me your blood pressure has returned to normal and that you are fit enough to travel. I've decided to give in to your pleadings and allow you to visit your godparents in Cordoba. I will drive you there this afternoon."

"*¡Tío!*" Carmen's joyous cry rang throughout the dining room and Rachel had the impression the younger woman would have jumped up from the chair to hug her uncle. But his next words checked her movements and some of her color receded.

"The doctor also told me you need a rest from the baby. He feels a few days, a week perhaps, to sleep in to your heart's content, to stay out with friends and enjoy yourself without having to be held to Luisa's rigid schedule, will be beneficial in effecting a full recovery after your long confinement.

"Since Miss Ellis is hoping the police will be able to locate her brother before she must return to the States, I've asked her to stay at the house and care for Luisa in your absence. It's a temporary solution for all of us. I have weighty business matters in Morocco that need my attention, and I'll feel better knowing that while you and I are both away, Luisa is in the best of hands with her aunt."

Rachel couldn't understand why the announcement about his business trip should make her feel such an unexpected sense of loss. As for Carmen, her eyes glistened with tears.

"But, *Tío,* my godparents have been begging to see how grown up Luisa has become. I want to show her off to them, t-to everyone." She buried her face in her hands.

A strange look entered the *señor*'s eyes, one Rachel couldn't decipher. "Not this time, *chica.*" That underlying note of authority was in his voice, signaling that there would be no more discussion on the subject.

Wanting to comfort the younger woman, Rachel leaned forward. "Carmen," she murmured in an unsteady voice, "I love Luisa like my own. She's a part of Brian, therefore a part of me. I swear I'll take perfect care of her for you. If it will help, you can phone me any time of the day or night. I'll put the receiver to Luisa's ear and you can talk to her so she knows you're right there for her."

Her dark head came up and she stared straight at Rachel. "You would do that?"

Through the veil of heavy black lashes that made his eyes so extraordinary, the *señor* flashed Rachel a look of intense gratitude mixed with some other emotion she didn't understand, but it filled her with inexplicable excitement.

"Of course," she answered Carmen more slowly and finally tore her eyes from his. "If Luisa were mine, I'd have a hard time leaving her, too. But I've done enough baby tending to know that even the healthiest new mother needs an occasional break from her duties. Babies may be adorable, but they're also demanding."

Carmen appeared to consider what Rachel said, then pushed herself away from the table. Getting to her feet, she faced her uncle, her back rigid with determination.

"I'll go to my godparents today, *Tío,* but if you think I'm going to start seeing Raimundo again, then you don't understand me at all. I love Brian and I always will." On that defiant note, she ran from the room.

"Don't be overly concerned about Carmen, Miss Ellis." The *señor* must have read her mind because though she had no right to interfere, she wanted to go after his niece and reassure her. "Progress has been made, and I owe it all to you. You handled her perfectly." His gaze wandered intently over Rachel's features before he drained his wineglass.

While part of her trembled, another part bristled at what she considered a left-handed compliment, as if she'd intentionally tried to manipulate Carmen. "I meant everything I said, *señor.*"

"I never doubted it," came the mild rebuke. "Neither did she, or she wouldn't have agreed to go at all," he added succinctly.

The maid chose that moment to serve them a pastry dessert. Rachel waited until she'd left the room before bringing up the subject foremost on her mind. "Does this Raimundo live in Cordoba?"

"*Sí.*"

When nothing else was forthcoming, she ventured, "It won't work, you know. Carmen is too much in love with Brian to look at another man, *señor.* Women are like that."

"Do you honestly think that most men are any different from a woman in that regard?" he demanded cooly. In a heartbeat, their conversation had turned into something personal and disquieting.

Rachel lowered her fork, wondering if he had been thinking of his own marriage which evidently had been a real love match. If that were the case, then his emotions were still raw where Leonora's memory was concerned. Shattered by that possibility she said, "I only meant th—"

"It's perfectly clear what you meant, *señorita*. But be careful you do not use your..." He paused, and she thought it was deliberate. "Father's and brother's behavior as the standard by which you compare all men."

Curiously enough, it was the lesson she'd learned from Stephen which had prompted her remark. Odd how distanced she felt from him now.

Since her arrival in Spain, she no longer experienced the attendant pain she'd felt at the beginning. The most emotion she could dredge up was a healthy sense of disgust for having gotten involved with him in the first place.

Afraid to be alone any longer with the man who in two days had transformed her life so she didn't recognize it, she thanked her host for the delicious meal, and started to get up. But a firm hand closed over hers, preventing her from leaving, sending a river of heat through her body which he could probably feel.

She had an idea that if she tried to escape, she would know the full strength of those long, suntanned, well-shaped fingers entrapping hers until she cried out for mercy.

"Anyone watching would think you were trying to run away from me," he mocked before letting her go. "However, if that were true, then you wouldn't have accepted a position in my household in the first place, which must mean you're eager to play nanny to my little niece."

"Naturally I'm anxious to get acquainted with her," Rachel agreed quickly, not only out of a sense of self-preservation, but because on some level she felt he was still suspicious of her where Brian was concerned.

"Then before you disappear, I'd like to discuss the terms of your employment. First of all, I don't expect you to be on duty twenty-four hours a day. When Luisa is napping or down for the night, you will be free to do as you wish. If you need to shop or want to sightsee, Felipe will be at your disposal."

"Thank you, *señor*," she murmured, breathing too hard, "but since I won't be in Spain longer than a week, I won't be needing anything."

"Be that as it may, from time to time unforeseen emergencies can and do arise. Simply charge them to my account and I'll deduct them from your wages. *¿Es claro?*"

She nodded without meeting his eyes. "Yes, of course."

"Felipe always knows where to reach me and will get the doctor on the phone should there be the slightest problem with Luisa. *Mi casa es su casa, señorita.* Treat it as your own home. On my way out, I'll ask Maria to show you to your room. It is next to Carmen's suite so that you will be able to hear Luisa if she needs you in the night. Do you have any questions?"

"Not a question exactly, but I do need to phone the States and understand that it's cheaper to pay for the calls from this end. I'll ask the operator to give me the cost after each phone call and pay you when I leave, if that's all right.''

He unexpectedly pushed himself away from the table and stood up, his powerful body looming over hers. ''I'd take your money right now. Unfortunately I have pressing matters and can't spare the time for you to go in search of your purse, so we'll have to settle this vital issue at a later date,'' he snapped with heavy sarcasm, letting her know she had offended him.

Upon reflection she realized that he was unused to dealing with independent women who didn't look to a man for their livelihood, who expected to pay their own way.

''Señor Riano,'' she called after him and jumped up from the table, anxious to explain that she hadn't meant to be rude. But he was out of the room before she could catch up with him. In the next instant Maria appeared in the doorway, ready to escort Rachel upstairs.

Feigning calm, she followed the maid to the elegant suite furnished in rich blue and gold brocade which would be her home for the next little while. Beneath the surface her emotions were in such turmoil she didn't know where to turn, let alone find the courage to analyze them.

''*SEÑORITA* ELLIS? The telephone. The *patrón* wishes to speak to you.''

Rachel had heard the phone ring and assumed it was Carmen making her nightly call to inquire about Luisa before going to bed. Somehow Rachel hadn't expected to talk to the *señor* who hadn't made an appearance since he'd driven his niece to Cordoba four days earlier. She resented the fluttery feeling in the pit of her stomach just because his name was mentioned.

"Thank you, Maria."

She handed the maid the empty bottle and put Luisa to bed for the night, explaining to Maria as she lay the baby on her back that this was a fairly recent technique proven to help prevent infant crib death.

After covering her with a light blanket and kissing her good-night, she hurried to the phone at Carmen's bedside table, conscious of unsteady fingers as she picked up the receiver.

"Hello?" To her consternation she sounded out of breath.

"Rachel?" came the distinctive voice of her host, pronouncing her name with the merest trace of accent which made her heart turn over. "You don't mind my calling you that? After all, we're practically related." Any hint of his earlier irritation was gone.

Her mouth went dry as cotton. She tried moistening her lips, to no avail. "No. Of course not, *señor.*"

"Then you shouldn't have a problem calling me Vincente. *¿Verdad?*"

She hardly knew how to respond. "Another time and I'll try to remember."

"Perhaps after tomorrow evening you won't have such a struggle," he countered dryly.

A shivery feeling raced down her spine. "Tomorrow evening? I—I don't understand."

"This is your first visit to Spain, is it not?"

Her hand tightened on the receiver. "Yes."

"Then, as your host, I would be remiss if I didn't treat you to an evening of flamenco, something for which Seville is renowned throughout the world."

A frisson of excitement quickened her body. "You hired me to tend Luisa, *señor*. I promised Carmen I would be here day and night."

"That was a rash promise, *pequena,* one you are not required to keep."

Pequena? She didn't know that word.

"Maria served as a part-time nanny to Carmen after she was born and is perfectly capable of looking after Luisa for a few hours." There was a slight pause. "Even our cruel Spanish laws dictate that the hired help be given a day off from their weekly duties," he mocked.

"Yes, but if Carmen should—"

"When and if my niece calls," he interrupted suavely, "Maria will deal with it. I'm still in Rabat on business, but will return in time to escort you. Be ready to leave for dinner by seven-thirty.

"In case you didn't pack any evening wear, I've arranged to have several dresses delivered from Carmen's favorite shop tomorrow morning. Hopefully you'll see something that pleases you. Now I must ring off. *Buenas noches,* Rachel."

"*Señor?* Vincente?" she cried out in exasperation. "Wait—"

But the line had gone dead.

Filled with too many conflicting emotions, it took her a minute to realize she'd forgotten to put the receiver back on the hook.

The idea of going anywhere socially with Vincente de Riano was ludicrous. She was his employee, for heaven's sake! One, furthermore, who was attempting to pay off Brian's debt.

Brian...

She closed her eyes. Because she was Brian's sister, most likely the *señor* assumed she was motivated by greed, the same as her brother, and if given the opportunity would grab at anything freely offered. Maybe this was some sort of test...

But even if the *señor* had no ulterior motives in providing her with evening clothes, did he honestly think she'd wear something he'd bought for her? Perhaps that sort of thing was done among his coterie of friends, but she wasn't a part of his affluent world and despised women who used men like that.

Disturbed by the conversation more than she wanted to admit, Rachel checked on the baby one more time, then went to her own room and phoned Liz who lived in her same apartment building, explaining about her change in plans.

Liz, in turn, told Rachel that Stephen would really be upset when he found out she wasn't coming home right away, that she'd found another job despite his efforts to sabotage her references.

After finding her resignation in his box at the hotel, he'd practically gone out of his mind and admitted to Liz that he'd said and done a lot of stupid things because he was angry and wanted Rachel back. According to Liz, the man was in hell and threatened to come to Spain to take her home.

Though Liz's words provided a balm to Rachel's injured pride, they didn't touch her heart because Stephen wasn't capable of a lasting relationship. In fact he was probably in bed with someone else right now, consoling himself.

The entire time Liz was talking, Rachel kept wondering about the *señor,* what he was doing, if he was asleep, how he entertained himself away from Seville.

A seering pain shot through her when she considered the possibility that he might be attempting to assuage his grief and loneliness in another woman's arms....

Terrified at the implication, Rachel thanked Liz for keeping her informed, but made it clear that it was over with Stephen.

After thanking her friend for watering the plants in her apartment and passing on the phone messages—none of which to her bitter disappointment were from Brian—Rachel promised to call again soon, then rang off.

All the while they'd been talking, she'd half listened for Luisa who, according to Carmen, occasionally woke up during the night and wanted to be held. However, all was silent for the moment.

After getting ready for bed, Rachel reached for a sack in her tote bag containing a couple of novels she'd bought at the airport before leaving New York. Something to read on the plane.

But after boarding her flight, her excitement over the impending reunion with Brian had prevented Rachel from concentrating on much of anything. She never even looked at the titles.

Now was her chance. She'd been wanting to read the latest bestseller. But when the first paragraph didn't hold her, she knew it was hopeless and closed the book, setting it on the bedside table.

Damn Vincente de Riano for phoning her this late at night and disturbing her peace of mind. *Damn* the chemistry that electrified her body whenever he was around, making her ache to touch him even during their most heated confrontations.

What truly upset her was that even now, when he was many miles away in North Africa, the timbre of his deep voice continued to waft over her nerve endings like a warm desert wind, making her come alive and expectant. *And for what?*

Certainly not for any fantasy her mind might be conjuring up in the long dark hours of the night! Hadn't she learned anything from Stephen's betrayal?

She was the sister of Brian Ellis, her host's alleged enemy. If the *señor* had invited her to experience Seville's nightlife, then it was a calculated move on his secret agenda to discover her vulnerabilities and play on them for the information he thought she harbored.

She'd be a fool to read anything else into it.

Too keyed up to fall asleep, Rachel threw back the covers, slipped on her robe, and padded into the next apartment. Right now she needed comfort from one golden-haired little girl whose warm body might bring the needed calm to Rachel's troubled spirit.

No sooner had she sat down in the chair and cuddled a sleepy Luisa in her arms than Maria, also in a robe, made an appearance in the alcove. Her eyebrows lifted in silent query. "Something is wrong?" she whispered.

"No," Rachel murmured, shaking her head. "I just felt like holding her."

The older woman smiled. "You watch over her like her own mama."

"I love her."

"Everyone in this house loves the *pequena*."

"Explain that word to me."

She shrugged her shoulders. "*Niña*. Little one."

Little one. The *señor* had used that endearment with Rachel on the phone earlier. *Why?* What did it mean? What did she *want* it to mean?

At that instant her body shivered, waking the baby who yawned luxuriously, then opened her eyes. Such beautiful black eyes, reminiscent of another pair of dark, smoldering orbs whose inner fire had already licked at the core of Rachel's ragged emotions and threatened to create an inferno if she drew any closer.

"The *niña* no longer sleeps. I will bring another bottle."

Fathoms deep in thought, Rachel's head swerved guiltily at the sound of Maria's voice. She stammered her thanks, then put Luisa back in bed to change her diaper, all the while cognizant of the frightening conviction that as long as she stayed in the *señor*'s house, in his country, Rachel would never find rest.

If only there were some way to track down Brian before she became any more emotionally involved with her host. It didn't seem decent that already Vincente de Riano had supplanted Stephen in her thoughts.

Perhaps if she paid another visit to the monastery and talked to the abbot... Maybe he could tell her something of Brian's habits, how he used to spend his free time. He might remember a detail which would provide her with a lead.

Her thoughts raced ahead. The *señor* was still away in Morocco, and so far the baby had been consistent in sleeping from about twelve to three each day....

If at noon tomorrow Rachel asked Felipe to drive her into town and leave her until she phoned to be picked up again, she could rent a car, drive to La Rabida and be back home in time to take care of Luisa after she awakened. No one would be the wiser and she might learn something that would help her find Brian.

Unfortunately, the best laid plans had a way of not working out. When the next day arrived and Rachel told the staff to refuse any packages sent out by the *señor* which would be arriving shortly, she apparently upset the entire household. Maria waved her hands in the air and said that none of them would take responsibility for such an act.

To make matters worse, Rachel left for La Rabida only to discover that the abbot was away in Madrid on church business. She would have to travel there again in another week's time when he had returned because none of the other priests had been acquainted with Brian.

Needing to work off her dejection, she returned to the house, refused her tea tray, and took Luisa out to the garden at the back of the house for the rest of the afternoon.

The worst heat of the day had passed and Luisa seemed to thrive in the outdoors while she sucked happily on bottled water. More often than not, Rachel held the baby in her arms while they walked beneath the refreshing shade of the palms, thoughts of the *señor* and Brian going around and around in her head until she lost all track of time.

When one of the house maids came out to the garden and informed her that the *señor* had returned from his trip and expected her to join him in the study before they went out to dinner, Rachel panicked.

She was afraid to be alone with him, afraid of her attraction to him and his uncanny powers of discernment. On impulse she sent her apologies via the maid, explaining that Luisa needed her and she'd decided to stay in for the evening.

As soon as the shocked maid hurried off with the message, Rachel purposely began making elaborate preparations for Luisa's bath. Knowing she would get splashed because Carmen told her the baby loved water, Rachel wore her favorite T-shirt of the Knicks and coiled her braid around the top of her head.

Secretly she hoped that if the *señor* came looking for her, he would be put off by the casual attire no proper

Spanish woman would be caught dead in, and cancel their evening out.

Not five minutes later her assumption was born out when she heard a deep, familiar voice say, "I doubt the *patrón* of the Malaguena would allow you inside dressed like that for fear you would start a riot."

Rachel shouldn't have peered over her shoulder. The *señor*'s powerful frame filled the bathroom doorway. He looked impossibly dark and handsome in a mid-night blue dress suit.

She swallowed hard in reaction, wondering when he'd entered Carmen's apartment, how long he'd been watching her at the sink. Somehow she hadn't counted on the way his eyes wandered intimately over the curves of her body outlined by the wet T-shirt, nor the way his interested gaze followed the line of her long, slender legs, bare beneath the ragged fringe of her cutoffs.

"I'll finish up here while you get ready," he murmured huskily. Before she could countenance it, he'd removed his suit coat, hung it on the door handle, and had started toward her with a fluffy blue towel in hand.

Averting her eyes, she had no choice but to lift Luisa out of the water and deposit the wiggly body in her uncle's waiting arms.

Not bothering about his fabulous white dress shirt or the navy-and-silver-striped tie, he hugged Luisa against his heart and wrapped her in the towel, whispering Spanish endearments and pressing little kisses in the sweet curve of her neck.

Rachel could just imagine how that would feel against her own sensitized skin, and a moan escaped.

Too late she realized he might have heard her and she started to slip past the two of them. But she only made it as far as the door before he turned around and pinned her with a glittery gaze that filled her with unease.

"Maria tells me you wouldn't open the packages sent out from the shop."

"That's right." Though her heart pounded crazily, she stood her ground. "I don't need any evening clothes because I'm not going out with you. I presume it is your Spanish blood that produces this strange code of honor which drives you to keep me entertained, while at the same time exacting the debt Brian owes you by making me responsible for Luisa's care."

She paused for breath and hated the way a slow smile broke the corner of his sensual mouth, haunting her with his male beauty. "Any way you analyze it, I'm a mere employee like Maria or Sharom. I would appreciate it if you would treat me as such."

"That would be impossible," he declared, undaunted. "You're Luisa's aunt, which puts you in an entirely different category than the staff. Perhaps I failed to mention that the chief of police and his wife are among my closest friends. They will be joining us for drinks before the show."

Rachel's eyes widened at that revelation.

"I thought you'd like an opportunity to discuss your brother's case with him. Hernando is a congenial man and he'll be happy to answer any questions that are troubling you. In all probability, he'll find your defense of Luisa's father as compelling as I do."

CHAPTER SIX

EVERY TIME SHE THOUGHT she understood her host, he said or did something that confused her to the point that she didn't know how to respond. The more time she spent in his company, the more complicated the issues tended to become.

"Couldn't you invite them here for drinks?" she asked quietly.

"Of course." By this time he'd powdered Luisa and put on her diaper and undershirt. "But it has been a long time since I enjoyed an evening out," he admitted in a low voice, sounding far away, "and though I'm no longer officially in mourning, I'd prefer to escort someone close to the family who neither wants nor expects anything from me, if you understand my meaning."

After a quiet interval Rachel nodded, very much afraid that she did. Suddenly her world had turned desolate.

"Relax, Rachel. You may stay home if you prefer, but if you are worried about a phone call from Carmen, you don't need to be. Not five minutes ago I was speaking with her and explained that we would be going out. She understands that you need a rest from responsibilities which you've carried out far beyond anyone's expectations. My household is buzzing with excitement over the care you're giving Luisa. It's obvious she thrives on your affection."

"She's easy to love," Rachel whispered, shocked by the compliment when only a few days ago he'd been so enangered by her appearance at his villa, he couldn't get rid of her soon enough.

How, in the short time since she'd known him, had the situation changed so drastically that she would feel churlish if she refused his invitation? One arranged for *her* benefit as much as his? Apparently he was still in love with his wife's memory, a reality which disturbed Rachel more than it should have.

"I—I brought a basic black dress which I can dress up with accessories. I'll hurry."

Fitting Luisa's tiny feet into her stretchy suit, he murmured, "If you wear your hair down, you'll need no other adornment. But you must suit yourself. Perhaps it's an element in your American blood that makes you perverse."

"Perverse?" she shot back from the doorway.

"Isn't that the word to describe a woman who says no when she means yes?"

Right now he had centered all his attention on Luisa. "Let us hope, *pequena,* that *you* haven't inherited the same trait as your aunt. Otherwise, wherever you go, you will create mass chaos among the many men who will desire a relationship with you."

Chuckling deep in his throat, he raised her in the air to give her rounded tummy some more kisses.

Rachel couldn't bear to watch or listen any longer and fled to her bedroom, a trembling mass of conflicting emotions.

She took a quick shower, then dressed in the sleeveless silk jersey with its flared skirt. A few minutes later, when she sat down at the dressing table to do her hair, his mocking remarks about her contrary nature came back to haunt her.

Normally she would wear her hair down, but only if she had just shampooed it to make it smooth. Since there wasn't time to wash it, she'd have to come up with another solution because wearing it in a braid had put crinkles in it.

Frustrated because of indecision which had its roots in the *señor's* remarks, she finally opted to wear it in its usual style and swept it back from her face in a twist which she secured with two pearl picks to match her earrings.

Other than a frosted pink lipstick, Rachel disliked makeup. Her eyebrows and lashes didn't need darkening. If anything, the hectic color in her cheeks ought to be toned down with a little powder, but she hadn't brought a compact with her.

Perfume happened to be her weakness and she sprayed on a little Fleurs De Rocaille which Stephen had given her on her birthday. After their breakup, her first inclination had been to throw it out along with the other gifts he'd given her throughout their six-month courtship.

But at the last minute she reconsidered, and decided that tossing away good French perfume gave Stephen

more importance than he deserved, so she kept it. Now
she was glad.

Because of the warm nights, she wouldn't need a
wrap, only her evening bag. On her way out the door
she slipped her feet into black sling-back pumps, then
hurried to Carmen's apartment to check on Luisa one
more time and give Maria instructions.

Five minutes later, she started down the elegant
marble staircase, then hesitated before continuing because the *señor* stood at the bottom. He was watching
her descent through eyes that gleamed like banked
fires.

Her heart took up its ridiculous hammering again.
Summoning inner strength, she forced herself to concentrate so she could finish that long walk, aware of his
gaze playing over her face and curves. He appeared
fascinated by the way the dress molded to her hips, then
flared to dance around her long, shapely limbs with
every step. He'd given her that same look in the bathroom while she was bathing Luisa, and it had turned
her limbs to liquid.

Rachel had heard that Latin men couldn't help
making every woman they met feel desirable, whether
she were nine or ninety. Of course her host meant
nothing by it, but more than ever Rachel could understand why he needed a buffer against unwanted female attention when he went out in public. He made
every male she'd ever known fade into insignificance.

Instinctively she knew something else... Vincente de
Riano was a man who liked to do the chasing. Any
woman foolish enough to press her unwanted atten-

tion on him, especially while he was still grieving for his dead wife, would be writing out her own death sentence.

Gearing up to withstand another acerbic comment, he surprised her once more by remarking sotto voce, "*Gracias, pequena.* You are the first woman of my acquaintance not to keep me waiting half the night. For this I am in your debt."

At the use of that word again, her heart turned over. It didn't matter that she'd just been lecturing herself on the futility of a woman trying to win the *señor*'s affection. Right now all she could think about was what he would do if she suddenly let go of her inhibitions and touched her lips to his firm jaw, the tiny cleft of his chin, his enticing mouth...

Terrified she might not be able to stop herself from acting on those impulses, she blurted out, "Shouldn't we be going?"

Without waiting for a response, she hurried toward the front doors, half in fear, half in sick excitement because she'd be spending the rest of the evening with him.

"Tell me about your day," he asked once he'd helped her inside the back seat of the Mercedes and instructed Felipe to start the car.

Tell me about your day. For the *señor* to say something so out of character made Rachel want to laugh out loud. Felipe would already have informed him she'd gone into town on the pretext of doing a little sight-seeing. Her host's conversational tone didn't fool her the tiniest bit, and in nervous anticipation of what was coming next, she hugged her side of the door, far too aware of him to relax.

A nagging voice said that now would be the time to tell him the exact nature of her trip, but she was loathe to broach the subject because the *señor* wouldn't stop his interrogation until he had a full-blown explanation of her activities. She felt it would be better to leave Brian's name out of the conversation until she had some pertinent news that could change the situation in some way.

Deciding to keep to a safer topic she started by saying, "I played with Luisa all morning. She's very responsive and alert for eight weeks. You can tell Carmen has been a devoted mother. It shows in dozens of ways." All the while she talked, she could feel his unswerving gaze on her and she gripped the armrest more tightly.

"Doesn't your job ever make you yearn for a child of your own?"

She'd been anticipating some kind of verbal attack. His unexpected question threw her off base so that she blurted out emotionally, "More than anything in the world." When she realized how that must have come across, she added, "In due time, of course."

"*In due time*. That's an interesting choice of words," came the wry insertion. "That could mean anything from a few days to fifty years."

"Well you can't have a baby without first having a husband!"

Deep, full-bodied laughter filled the plush interior, making the *señor* sound almost young and carefree.

She didn't know he could sound like that and it revealed another dimension to his fascinating character, one she would remember long after she'd returned to the States. . . . Already she could tell how bleak her life would be without his disturbing presence.

When the laughter subsided, he murmured, "You must be the last of an endangered species."

His comment brought her back to the present and her face went hot. "There are a few of us left."

"What a beguiling enigma you are, Rachel Ellis. As prim as an innocent novice on the inside, yet liberated enough to have rented a car today in a strange country and go off on your own despite the inherent dangers you've been warned about, despite the assertion that your funds are almost depleted."

In a heartbeat the fragile rapport between them disintegrated. She jerked her head around, the purple of her eyes darkening to pitch. "So *that's* why you made Felipe available to me, hoping to lay a trap, knowing you could count on his loyalty. He'd do anything for you, wouldn't he? Even to spying for you!" she cried out icily, forgetting that the man in question was chauffeuring them.

With a calmness she could scarcely credit, her host answered, "Felipe had nothing to do with a phone call from the rental agency where you left a plastic wallet holding several hundred dollars' worth of traveler's checks lying on the counter."

At his explanation, Rachel moaned in disbelief.

"Fortunately they had asked you for a local address and were able to report the missing money so you wouldn't be inconvenienced."

Like a magician, he produced the thin blue billfold containing her last two checks. Mortified to have been caught this way, she reached for the plastic wallet and was forced to feel the warmth of his fingers as she took it from him and put it in her purse.

She swallowed hard. "I'm sorry to have cast aspersions on Felipe. He's been very kind to me."

"I'm prepared to be kind to you, Rachel," he murmured in thick tones that stirred her senses alarmingly. "But you persist in seeing me as the ogre. If you had wanted a car to go sight-seeing, I would have provided you one. You had only to tell me."

Feeling guilty and defensive all at the same time she said, "You gave me the impression that when Luisa was asleep, my time was my own. Naturally in your absence I wouldn't presume on your generosity to that extent."

"Then I will make myself more available to you so that you'll be denied nothing which could add to the pleasure of being in my country while you tend our niece."

Rachel trembled at the implications, not only because she feared spending any more time alone with him, but because of the civility of his words which were a cloak for his anger over her refusal to give him a full explanation of her activities. He still didn't trust her and thought she had probably arranged some clandestine meeting with Brian.

Through tight lips she gibed, "I thought you had pressing business matters away from Seville, which was one of the main reasons I'd been hired to watch over Luisa."

"So I did. And because of your help, I was able to concentrate on a solution to a troublesome problem with my Moroccan distributors. Now we can leave for the villa in the morning and enjoy a small vacation."

They were going to Aracena?

Rachel started to panic. "I—I don't think—"

"Excuse me for interrupting," he broke in on her. Before she knew how it happened, he had undone her seat belt. Perhaps it was her imagination, but his fingers seemed to linger against the curve of her hip where she felt their burning intensity. "We arrived at our destination several minutes ago and will have to continue this conversation later. Hernando doesn't like to be kept waiting." As he slid his hand away from her silken thigh, Rachel gasped.

Her host couldn't help but witness her reaction and his mocking expression was replaced by a sharp look of concern. "*¡Por Dios,* Rachel!" he observed thickly. "You turned pale just now. Are you ill?" His black eyes searched her face relentlessly. "Is that the real reason you didn't want to come out with me tonight?" he demanded, sounding surprisingly anxious. "Perhaps I should take you to hospital. You're in a foreign country and it's not uncommon to pick up a local bug."

She shook her head and looked down at her hands. "It's nothing," she lied, thankful he assumed she was sick. Anything would be better than his guessing the truth about her feelings for him.

"Somehow I don't believe you. If you're not ill, then I can only assume you're hiding something from me."

Her head reared back. "Like the fact that I met with my brother while you were in Rabat?" she retorted.

His features took on a glacial quality. "Is that what you did?"

She let out a shuddering breath. "Why don't you call the monastery at La Rabida? I'm sure the priest in charge will be happy to tell you anything you want to know about my abortive visit to the abbot who happens to be in Madrid this week." On that emotional note, she flung open the door and jumped from the car, wanting to escape him.

But he moved with unnerving speed. By the time she'd reached the entrance of the Malageuna, he'd taken firm hold of her elbow and ushered her through the doors. In a deceptively quiet voice she heard him say, "I've visited with him several times myself, but he could shed no new light on your brother's whereabouts. I'm sorry you felt you couldn't have asked Felipe drive you there, and sorrier still that you didn't approach me in the first place."

"No you're not," she snarled, wishing he would let go of her arm. "You don't trust me any more now than you did when we first met." To her mortification, her voice shook.

After a tension-filled silence he said, "Your explanation still doesn't explain your pallor of a few minutes ago."

"I guess it's because I'm hungry," she dissembled. "At home I usually eat around five-thirty, and I'm not used to dining so late."

Lines marred his dark features. "That's why we serve tea. Sharom told me you refused your afternoon tray."

"That's because Sharom's lunches are so filling. But from now on I promise I'll have tea like everyone else. Then I won't suffer from hunger pains, because that's all they are. I swear it," she assured him, raising earnest violet eyes in unconscious pleading, not wanting him to guess at the root of her turmoil.

His hand tightened against her flesh. *"Rachel—"* Her name came out on a ragged whisper, as if he'd reached the limit of his endurance.

"Vincente!" A masculine voice spoke from directly behind them. Rachel broke free and with flushed cheeks whirled around while her host introduced her to the police chief and his wife standing at the bar.

"Vincente tells me this is your first trip to Spain, Señorita Ellis." His dark eyes played over her features in male admiration. "How do you like it so far?"

"I find your country enchanting, Señor Vasquez. History has come alive for me. Every kilometer of ground, every castle and church has a story to tell."

"Beautifully put," he murmured in heavily accented English, nodding his approval. A big, handsome man in his early fifties, he wore a mustache and was silvering at the temples. "Try an hors d'oeuvre, *señorita.*"

Rachel took one look at the raw fish rolled up with a toothpick, its little hairs still protruding from their pores, and her stomach rebelled at the sight of it. The drink Hernando passed to her was just as bad. One sip and she thought she would be sick on the spot.

"You must give the Americana more time to acclimatize, Hernando," her enigmatic host intervened with a chuckle, his dark attraction even more pronounced within the shadowy light of the Malaguena's celebrated barrel bar.

"I happen to know ham and cheese *tapas* are more to her liking. As for sangria, orange juice and sherry are an acquired taste, *compadre*. A hearty Valdepeña would suit her better. Here. Try this, Rachel."

She eagerly took the glass of wine her host extended and swallowed a larger amount than normal, thankful to discover its sweet flavor washed away any traces of the other.

"Thank you."

She avoided his eyes which refused to leave hers when when she dared an occasional glimpse at him.

Señora Vasquez laughed softly and patted Rachel's arm. "Pay no attention to my husband, Señorita Ellis. This is his favorite joke which he always enjoys playing on foreigners. Be good, *mi esposa*," she warned her husband in a tone of mock severity. The older man flashed his wife a devilish grin.

Rachel warmed at once to the older couple and discovered that she'd lost some of her initial nervousness. "Señor Vasquez, I realize that the reason we're all here is because of my brother, Brian."

She took a steadying breath. "Though it's very hard for me to believe he has done anything criminal, I would be a fool if I didn't admit to the possibility. I— I've made some inquiries at the American embassy and they've suggested several people who would provide legal counsel for Brian once he's in custody. H-he needs to be found right away." Her voice quivered. "I have to return to the States as soon as possible. If there is anything I can do to help while I'm still here, I will."

He pursed his lower lip. "If it is any consolation, *señorita,* the abbot at La Rabida believes in your brother's innocence. Like you, he is of the impression that your brother has run away because he is frightened."

Unable to help herself, Rachel's glance slid to the *señor* who stared at her with unsmiling eyes. It confused her that he had been scrupuously fair in relating everything she'd told him about Brian to the police chief. With pounding heart, she looked away again.

"Perhaps if we had a picture of him which we could circulate among our various police precincts throughout the country, it is possible that someone might recognize him and turn him in. It would be for his own good."

"I agree. But I thought Señor de Riano had already given you a photograph." Her gaze flicked to her host's once more. "I don't understand. What about the picture you took from the packet in my room?" she asked with a hint of defiance. His stony expression puzzled her. "Do you still have it?"

The *señor* pushed his powerful body away from the bar and stood with his legs slightly apart. "You have made an incorrect assumption, *señorita,*" he answered impersonally. "The picture of you and your mother is now in the hands of a gifted artist friend of mine who is creating a life-size portrait. I wouldn't want Luisa to forget the American side of her heritage. It's important for a child to know who she is. Solid roots will make her feel more secure in an insecure world."

"What a perfectly beautiful gesture, Vincente." Señora Vasquez verbalized her approval along with her husband.

Rachel had no idea.... Flustered by so many conflicting emotions, she avoided the *señor's* piercing gaze and turned to the police chief. "I left my packet of pictures at Señor de Riano's, but I'll see that you get them right away. Of course, they were taken at least six years ago and a few are too old to be of any use to you."

He finished the last of his sangria. "At least they will give our artist several angles to work up a sketch. Vincente tells me you could be your brother's twin, so our job shouldn't be difficult."

The police chief must have noticed Rachel shiver because he said in a benign voice, "I will handle your brother's case personally, and see to it that justice is served one way or the other."

With a solemn nod Rachel answered, "I can't ask for more than that. You've been very understanding about everything. Thank you."

"It is my pleasure. Now let us go in and enjoy dinner and the show."

Avoiding the eyes of the *señor*, Rachel took the police chief's extended arm and they walked through an alcove to a somberly lit dining room. The whole time she was conscious of her host following suit with Señora Vasquez.

As Hernando showed Rachel to their places at one of the tables surrounding the wooden dance floor, he murmured, "I have to tell you it is good to see Vincente out again, even if he only came to get you and me together. Since you're family, Carmen has probably told you he buried his heart with his wife. Sometimes I think the little *niña* is all that he lives for these days. It is very sad."

Suddenly her host's earlier declaration that he would adopt Luisa if necessary added credence to Hernando's words. Devastated by the revelation, Rachel found herself swaying and had to cling to the back of the nearest chair for support.

Fortunately no one else seemed to notice and the arrival of dinner gave her something to do. Though her appetite had deserted her, she forced herself to eat so the *señor* wouldn't be any more suspicious of her behavior.

Unable to look at him without remembering Hernando's shattering words, Rachel turned to Señora Vasquez. While the two men talked quietly, she feigned enthusiasm and plied the older woman with a dozen questions about flamenco. As long as she didn't look in her host's direction, she thought she might be able to last until it was time to go home.

But when the spotlight focused on the man and woman who began their primitive dance to the haunting music, making the floor rock with their wooden heels, Rachel's blood picked up the rhythm and she felt as if she were suffocating with sensation.

While the man stood erect and rakish in the flat-crowned hat set at a jaunty angle so that the broad brim partially hid his Latin eyes, he watched the voluptuous sway of the woman's hips, felt the teasing ruffles of her dress around his whipcord legs as she made her passes, enticing, then retreating in the oldest love play of all.

Rachel found that she could scarcely breathe because it was Vincente's impossibly handsome face she saw beneath that hat—Vincente's strong, virile body that commanded the woman and drew her inexorably toward him with effortless male grace. She could imagine herself that woman, and knew she had never experienced anything so erotic in her life.

In the darkness, Rachel gave in to the compulsion she'd been fighting and darted a glance at her host, noting the dark, brooding expression marring his features. No doubt he was remembering moments of shared passion with his wife, which thought sent Rachel into a depression that made her want to run from the Malaguena, run from the feelings the *señor* aroused in her without his even being aware of them.

She'd known instinctively that this evening would end in disaster, which was why she'd fought so hard not to give in to him. But she hadn't counted on it wounding her to the very essence of her being.

Why didn't the music stop? The sensual beauty of the dance was nothing but pure torture to her now. She doubted she would ever be able to experience flamenco again without remembering the wretchedness of this night. To be reminded of how empty her life was going to be when the *señor* was no longer a part of it didn't bear thinking about.

With shocking certainty, she knew she'd fallen headlong in love with her host, the soul-wrenching, tormenting kind of love that had plagued her mother. *This* was the kind of love from which you never recovered....

CHAPTER SEVEN

RACHEL FELT TRAPPED. The last thing she wanted to do was drive to the villa with him in the morning—the place where he'd known happiness with Leonora—where they'd conceived a child. *Dear God.*

Suddenly Carmen couldn't come back from Cordoba soon enough to suit Rachel. For the first time in six years, bitter resentment over Brian's selfishness which had brought her to this untenable point threatened to taint her loving memories of him. She wished she'd never tried to find him, then she wouldn't have met Vincente de Riano!

"Señorita Ellis?"

So deep ran her agonizing thoughts, she didn't realize that the dancers had left the floor, or that the *señor* was talking to her. To her horror, the other two seemed to be looking at her with anxious eyes.

She finally braved a glance in his direction. "I'm sorry, *señor.* Did you ask me something?"

A grim expression wiped his striking features of animation, making him appear older. "It's obvious that other thoughts occupy your mind, not the least of which is the worry over your brother," he remarked cryptically.

Like a lifeline, Rachel grasped at his faulty supposition.

"I—I didn't mean to ruin this evening for any of you." She apologized to the Vasquez's. "Thank you for bringing me here. I've never seen anything so thrilling. But the fact is, I *am* preoccupied over Brian's disappearance. The sooner he is found, the better it will be for everyone concerned. I can't afford to stay away from New York much longer."

"*¿Compadre?*" The *señor* turned to the police chief. "If I know Señorita Ellis, she is anxious to get back home to her tiny charge. Be good enough to follow us to the house and I'm certain she will supply you with any pictures you need." Then his head swiveled around. "*¿Verdad, señorita?*" He stared pointedly at her, as aloof and unapproachable as he had been outside his stable at Aracena.

Once again she was crushed by the knowledge that he was still mourning his dead wife, that this evening out had been solely for Rachel's benefit. Slowly she nodded and glanced at the police chief. "Yes. Of course."

"Shall we go?" Her host's autocratic voice brought the evening to a close. When his hand moved familiarly to her elbow, Rachel's heart plummeted to her feet. She didn't want him to touch her. She didn't want him to come near her.

Within seconds they reached the car and the *señor* joined her in the backseat, his thigh brushing hers as he sat back against the leather upholstery. Rachel's heart pounded so unmercifully it hurt. Paranoid that her host could hear it, she inched away from him.

"Relax, Rachel," he said irritably. "I may feel uncivilized at the moment, but I don't make a habit of pouncing on defenseless females. However, there is something we need to discuss before we arrive at the house and you disappear to the nethermost regions."

"If it's about my trip to La Rab—"

"It's not," he declared swiftly. "This has to do with Carmen who is enjoying herself enough to go to her godparents' beach cottage in Benidorm on the coast. Some sun and fresh sea air will do her a world of good."

Rachel's pulse quickened in alarm. "How long does she intend to stay? What about Luisa?"

He shrugged his broad shoulders. "I have no idea. Did she say anything more to you, Felipe?" He addressed the driver who, to Rachel's mortification, must have seen and heard everything going on in the backseat of the car. But like any well-trained family retainer, he blended into the background so perfectly, she'd forgotten he was there.

"No, *patrón*. Only that she would phone you and Señorita Ellis as soon as they arrive there."

Her host turned to Rachel, his fiery gaze enveloping her until she could feel its heat.

"Does her change in plans constitute something of a problem for you? I doubt that it will entail more than a couple of days at most. My niece would never be able to stay away from Luisa longer than that. Naturally you will be paid handsomely for any inconvenience."

Yes, Rachel wanted to shout at him. *There's something of a problem. To spend another second, let alone another hour or day with you constitutes the greatest crisis of my life.*

"You make me out to be a very mercenary person, *señor.* If money were my first priority, I would have pursued any career other than that of a nanny. But I'd wager that even the great Señor de Riano with all your background and connections would be the slightest bit worried if you suddenly found yourself out of gainful employment and still owing a huge debt." Her voice quavered. "Which means I need to get home and find another job as soon as possible."

His features hardened. "Let's get something clear, shall we?" The voice of ice. "You insult me by suggesting that I would ask you to pay back the money stolen from my business. I'm returning your traveler's checks in the form of cash which I'll include with your salary."

He paused briefly before saying, "Any debt owing can be taken care of by your brother, if and when he makes an appearance and it is proven that he is guilty."

She shook her head in confusion, staring at him through dazed eyes. "Are you admitting that it's possible he didn't steal from you after all?"

His sardonic expression did little to reassure her. "I admit nothing. I simply wished to make it clear that I do not expect anything from you but to love Luisa and watch out for her welfare until Carmen returns."

Sucking in her breath she said, "And I wish to make it clear that I can only tend Luisa for a little while lon—"

"We're almost home." He cut her off before she'd finished, infuriating her as only he knew how to do. "Once we've gone inside and you've relieved Maria, send her to my study with the pictures. Then you are free to resume your duties.

"Don't forget that we'll be leaving for Aracena in the morning. Seven-thirty *exactamente*. Maria will see to Luisa's things. What personal packing you need to do ought to be taken care of before you retire. When you're ready, inform Felipe and he'll carry your cases down to the car."

She assumed he'd finished dictating his orders and interjected with false calm, "I need to make another overseas phone call, if that's all right."

"*¡Por Dios*, Rachel!" he thundered, his emotions as violent as hers, if the whiteness of his knuckles from the fist he'd made against his rock-hard thigh was any indication. "You think me such a monster that you have to check with me every time you wish to speak to your lover?" he stormed, hot with anger.

Rachel recoiled from his outburst, thunderstruck by another one of his incorrect assumptions. "I've already told you that I don't—"

"*¡Basta!*" he ordered in Spanish. "You owe me no explanation."

She hadn't thought he could make her any angrier, but she was wrong. "And thus the king has spoken," she mocked with pleasure. "So far, everything you've done has only managed to reinforce my initial impression of you."

"And what was that?" His voice grated, sending chills through her body.

"That your arrogant, dictatorial ways are the perfect match for your uncompromising jaw and forceful chin." Which was not altogether a lie. "After seeing your ancestor's portrait in the upstairs hall, I concede that you've come by those traits honestly, but I don't profess to like them."

She regretted her words the second they left her lips, and was shocked by her own candid daring. But more shocking still was the *señor*'s reaction. Once again he threw back his head and laughed, the kind of rich laughter she loved to hear come out of him. That made twice in one evening. She had no idea he could let himself go that way.

"You may laugh, *señor,*" she muttered primly, still awed by this totally unexpected and beguiling side of his nature, "but I'm not the only person with the same opinion. Carmen has made herself quite clear on the subject. Fortunately she will be back in a few days and I will be able to leave your house before my wicked Ellis genes put another blight on your family's impeccable escutcheon."

Like quicksilver, his mood altered. In its wake, she felt something ominous emanate from the man at her side. As soon as the car came to a stop in front of the mansion, Rachel alighted from the backseat and ran inside the house. Her torment was too great to care that the Vasquez vehicle had pulled up behind them or that they had witnessed her flight and would speculate on the reasons why.

What they didn't know was that just sitting next to the *señor* in the back of his car was pure torture to her now, that the burning ache in her loins signaled a growing need to know his possession.

Carmen wouldn't be coming home for a while. Rachel doubted she could survive that long in this kind of agony. She'd never experienced such intense desire before.

Though she'd once enjoyed kissing Stephen, she'd thought that he'd spoken the truth when he said that her worry over Brian had locked up her emotions, thus preventing her from finding ultimate expression with a man.

But the short journey from the paddock to the patio in Vincente de Riano's arms the first day of her arrival in Spain had destroyed that myth for all time.

Not stopping to change, Rachel headed straight for Carmen's room where she found Luisa sound asleep on her back, just the way she'd left her several hours earlier.

"You're a little poppet, you know that?" she whispered to her adorable niece who'd become so dear to her she didn't know how she would tear herself away when the time came to fly home, which would be in a few more days.

Though frantic with anxiety because it meant that she'd have to try to function normally around her taciturn host for a little while longer, Rachel couldn't very well refuse to help out Carmen who was probably enjoying the respite from her rigorous routine more than she'd anticipated.

The *señor*'s biting reminder that the whole point of the exercise was to give his niece a much needed rest had served to silence Rachel's unspoken refusal. With great misgivings she had acceded to her host's request, knowing instinctively that she would have to fortify herself further against him by staying out of his way as much as possible.

But to her consternation, there was another part of her that was sinfully excited to be going to his villa for a few more days.

As soon as Maria made an appearance in the doorway, Rachel, who was swamped with ambivalent feelings of joy and guilt, tore herself away from the baby long enough to get the photographs, realizing that the police chief was downstairs with the *señor*, waiting for them.

The second the maid disappeared from the room with the packet, Rachel hurried to the phone to call Liz, anxious to find out if there'd been any word from Brian. It was *his* fault that she was in Spain at all, *his* fault that she'd fallen hopelessly in love with a man whose heart was about as accessible to her as the far side of the universe.

"RACHEL?"

At the sound of the *señor*'s deep, mesmerizing voice, Rachel stirred and her eyelids fluttered open to gaze into a pair of fiery black eyes wandering shamelessly over her face through the open window of his car.

A tide of heat swept through her body and she came fully awake, realizing that after tossing and turning a good part of the night, she'd slept nearly the whole way from Seville, lulled by the low, purring sounds of the motor.

Feeling embarrassed and vulnerable, she sat up with a start and brushed a lock of hair from her cheek which had escaped her hastily formed twist.

"Shall I carry you inside as I did Luisa, or—" his eyes traveled down her body "—are you capable of walking in on your own two legs?"

When he looked at her like that, she thought she'd faint and couldn't begin to read him. He didn't sound angry, but that could be a facade. After last night—

Needing to expend nervous energy, she looked all around her, aware that he'd brought the car to the back of the villa. "I'm sorry," she murmured, moistening her lips. "I hope Luisa didn't disturb you too much during the drive. You should have wakened me."

"It appears my Luisa takes after you rather than her own mother in that regard. She, too, fell asleep the moment we left the city limits."

"At least the drive was restful," she said, wishing he'd move away from the door. All she had to do was stretch her hand a few more inches and she'd be able to touch him.... "Our conversations always turn into a battleground. It must have been a nice change for you," she couldn't resist adding.

His eyes narrowed on her mouth. "Oddly enough, I enjoy our heated skirmishes. In fact I'm looking forward to more of your incendiary remarks this afternoon after Luisa goes down for her nap."

Her heart slammed into her ribs. "This afternoon?"

He finally opened the car door so she could get out. "After I've visited my office in Jabugo, I need to exercise my stallion. Have you ever been riding?"

She blinked, but it had nothing to do with the intense sunlight. "Yes. A few times. I'm still nervous around horses."

"You won't need to be with Paquita. She's a docile little mare made for a beginner like you. We'll ride through the forest where the air is cooler and eat a late lunch at the summit. The view will surprise you."

She closed her eyes to fight the excitement his words engendered and accompanied him across the back patio to the inside of the villa where a maid greeted them. "I—I don't have any clothes for riding."

"The T-shirt and shorts you were wearing while you bathed Luisa will be adequate, but if you prefer something that covers your legs, Carmen has an assortment of gear you can choose from. Catana will show you. Meet me at the stable at one. And, *señorita,* make sure you eat and drink something before we start out."

His warning held a wry inflection that turned her cheeks crimson. At the *señor*'s command, the maid motioned for Rachel to follow her to the upstairs apartments. Angry with herself because his absence always produced a hollow sense of loss, Rachel hurried up the steps, trying to remember that Luisa was the only reason she'd been brought to the villa in the first place.

The growing certainty that a reunion with her brother would never take place gnawed at her emotions even more. Under the circumstances she needed to get back to New York, a world so far removed from the *señor*'s both in culture and tradition, she could scarcely credit that they lived on the same planet.

While her thoughts churned, she happened to catch a glimpse of her host's tall figure striding through the tiled halls of the corridor bordering the swimming pool below. On impulse, she hid behind an arch where the bougainvillea trailed over the railing.

For a brief moment she needed to feast her eyes on him and noted the way he jerked his tie loose, raking his hands through his black hair as if something were disturbing him.

To Rachel, his slightly dissipated air only added to the intense attraction she felt for him. At the mansion in Seville he'd been the urbane host, often charming if not somewhat aggravating and dictatorial. But here at the villa he turned into a different person, moving about the house and grounds with restless, driven energy, almost like a hungry wolf on the prowl.

She assumed that the mercurial change in his demeanor resulted from the attendant memories of a fulfilled life with his adored wife which had been brutally cut off with the plane crash.

Afraid of being caught staring, Rachel moved on toward the suite of rooms reserved for Carmen and

Luisa, glad her niece was awake and needing attention.

While she pushed the baby in her swing, Rachel's gaze wandered repeatedly around the nursery. Whoever created the design had achieved a little corner of heaven, a peaceful, blissful haven of soft blue and white.

A pang of sadness enveloped her when she realized that this contemporary room with its furry animals and juvenile decor meant to delight any child, had been intended for the *señor*'s little boy. One whom fate denied him from ever seeing or holding....

When she couldn't stand the pain any longer, Rachel changed into her swimsuit, put a playsuit on the baby, and together they went down to the pool for a dip. Luisa seemed to love the water and for the next little while Rachel concentrated on her charge. She wasn't the only one to delight in the baby's reactions.

Before the morning was out, everyone on the *señor*'s staff had taken time to watch the *niña* swim and eat her rice cereal, their faces wreathed with broad smiles of love and affection for the little fair-haired *muchacha* who helped fill the big empty hole in the *señor*'s grieving heart.

Fortunately the water hid Rachel's tears. When she flew home, there'd be no *señor* to fill the yawning cavern of her own broken heart.

CHAPTER EIGHT

PAQUITA WAS A GENTLE, surefooted mount who followed the *señor*'s lead without problem. After ten minutes astride her, Rachel relaxed enough to enjoy the cooler mountain temperatures beneath the heavy canopy of leaves.

The *señor,* dressed in black, looked born to the saddle and led the way on his magnificent Arabian, giving Rachel a history lesson on the Moors which she found riveting.

Clearly the master, he kept his stallion under perfect control as they rode higher, but Rachel sensed the spirited animal would have loved to break loose if he'd been given his head.

After riding for close to half an hour, they came to a little clearing where the sun's rays penetrated the leaves enough to give the area a dappled effect. The *señor* dismounted and waited for her to catch up, his keen gaze taking in the picture she made wearing a white T-shirt and Carmen's form-fitting brown riding pants.

A little shiver raced down her spine when he looked at her like that. She was glad she hadn't worn her shorts after all.

When they'd first left the stable, he'd been preoccupied and remote, causing her to wonder if it was sorrow or work problems, or both, that weighed him down. But after a few minutes, he seemed to throw off his dark cloud and became the pleasant, congenial host, pointing out landmarks, patiently answering her many questions. From that point on, nothing had marred the rapport they shared, which was why his next question sent a little frisson of alarm through her body.

"How long had you been at the stables talking to Estaban before I arrived?"

"Fifteen minutes maybe." She tried to sound nonchalant as Paquita found some lush wild grass growing near a tiny stream running through the clearing. "His English is surprisingly good, much better than the other stable hands'."

"Not so surprising when you consider he worked in England for several years before I hired him to help groom the horses."

Rachel started to dismount. "He's very nice and offered to help translate for me in his free time when I go to Jabugo to make inquiries about my brother." She decided to admit the whole truth since the *señor* would discover her secret plans soon enough.

That's when she felt a firm pair of hands encircle her waist and help her to the ground. Because she was so stiff, Rachel was slightly unsteady on her feet and her back fell against the solid hardness of his chest.

"I assumed as much," he conceded. "Unfortunately, Estaban is also very married." The *señor* whispered the implicit warning against her tender neck, his hands biting into her sides with unmistakable pressure. "His wife is expecting her fourth child any minute now. While you are at the villa, it would be best if I accompany you wherever you want to go from here on out."

Furious at the implication, Rachel whirled around red-faced, but the action only brought her closer to him so that their thighs brushed against each other. When she tried to move, he locked her even tighter to him.

"If you're insinuating that I was purposely carrying on some kind of flirtation with him, you couldn't be more wrong. Luisa fell asleep sooner than I had anticipated, so I decided to get acquainted with Paquita before we went riding. I—I had no idea how well Esteban could communicate," she said in a breathless whisper, too aware of their closeness to think straight.

"I'm afraid Esteban is renowned for his great ability to communicate, much to his wife's grief."

Exploding with equal amounts of desire and indignation she blurted out, "Thank you for the warning, señor, but I'm not Carmen, and I'm well past the age where I need a father's protection or approval."

She felt his body stiffen. "While you are in my care, it would be best if you are not seen alone with him again. That way he will realize that you were only trying to make conversation, but that you did not mean to lead him on. I do not wish any more scandal to be connected with the de Riano name."

Livid, Rachel muttered, "I am not a de Riano, señor."

"Perhaps not in name, but you and I share an irrefutable bond through Luisa. One, perhaps, more binding than you know," he murmured cryptically.

Swallowing hard, as much from his nearness and the enticing male scent of his body as anything else, she said, "I did not invite Estaban's interest!"

"You didn't have to," he retorted. "The Latin male has no defense against your kind of beauty. It is up to the woman to steer the bull in the right direction."

Fire stormed her cheeks. "That's absurd. You put all the blame on the woman, as if a man is incapable of restraining himself. God endowed men and women with equal capabilities to hold their desire in check."

"But He did not create men and women equally," came the husky rejoinder. "Take a woman's skin, for example." Before she knew how it happened, he'd captured her right hand in the strong warmth of his. Feeling panicky, she tried to pull away from him, but he held her fast.

"Let us try an experiment, shall we?"

In the next instance he lifted her hand to her own face and forced her to feel the satiny smoothness of her skin.

Rachel's breath escaped in small pants. The brush of his fingers surrounding hers trailed fire along her flesh, igniting her senses. Her eyes closed involuntarily against the insidious onslaught of his sexuality.

"There is no softness comparable," he whispered in thick tones, his mouth achingly close to hers. "If you don't believe me, then feel the difference."

Drugged and confused, she went limp as he forced both her hands to his face, applying enough pressure for her to detect the slight rasp of his skin against her avid fingertips.

From the moment they'd met, she had yearned to touch the contours of his unforgettable face as she was doing now, yearned to drink in the intoxicating feel of his masculinity.

Slowly she lost awareness of her surroundings and was frightened she would succumb to the driving need to explore every inch of him.

"Touching me is not the same thing at all, is it?" he demanded silkily. "Can you look me in the eye, *señorita*, and tell me that God did not make it difficult, if not impossible, for a man to control himself in the face of such blatant temptation?"

He shook her with surprising force and only the primitive instinct to survive kept her from losing her head and meeting his fiery gaze.

Somehow she found the strength to pull out of his arms and weave her way over to the little mare where she gulped in stabilizing breaths of air.

"I'm still waiting for my answer," he persisted with that condescending smugness that provoked her because he'd assumed that he'd proven his point. In a twisted way, she supposed he had. The physical differences between a man and women were a universal truth, like night and day.

But did he honestly think a woman wasn't equally tempted by a man's superb physique, the lean tautness of his skin over a hard-muscled body, the contours of a noble face and proud forehead? How could she explain the exquisite feel of being carried in the warm, safe stronghold of his arms, of being crushed against his solidity where their blood caught fire from each other, and their hearts beat out one wild tattoo?

Afraid that if she stayed here another second, she would abandon all pride and throw herself at him, she did the next best thing and mounted Paquita, anxious to get as far away from the *señor* as possible.

He called to her but she ignored him and urged the mare forward, the anticipation of an intimate lunch and climb to the summit long forgotten in the tumult of emotions beyond her control.

At first she thought it was a clap of thunder that made Paquita jolt and started to gallop down the mountainside like a frightened rabbit. But the sound of the powerful stallion's hooves striking the ground in close pursuit revised her thinking.

With lightning speed the *señor* overtook her and reached across to grasp the reins, bringing the mare's headlong flight to a walk and eventual stop. Through the trees she could see the paved road and realized they weren't far from the stable now.

"*¡Madre de Dios,* Rachel!" he swore, white-lipped. "Whatever possessed you to take off like that?" he demanded, his breathing heavy and erratic. "Don't you know how close you came to breaking that beautiful neck of yours? Paquita was headed straight for the road. You could have been hit by a car!"

Rachel couldn't look at him and slumped over in the saddle, trembling with fright and relief. "I—I'm sorry. I never meant for this to happen."

He bit out another unintelligible epithet and leaped down from the saddle. "Stay mounted while I check El

Calife's hoof. He's favoring his left hind leg and gets skittish at a time like this. You're safer on Paquita."

The huge stallion snorted and quivered in place as the *señor* crooned in Spanish to his animal and forced the hoof from the ground to inspect it.

She wanted to ask him what he'd found but feared disturbing his concentration, so she remained silent. Several minutes went by while he worked at getting something pried loose. Suddenly the loud blare of a horn from a car rounding the curve rent the air.

Like a horrifying nightmare, she saw the stallion's leg kick out in reaction, knocking the *señor* to the ground.

"*Vincente*—" she screamed. Forgetting her own safety, she jumped down from her horse and ran over to him, unmindful of the stallion sniffing at his master while she sank into the grass to examine him.

A little blood oozed from the side of his head, matting his black hair near the temple. He didn't move.

"My darling *Vincente*—" she cried out again, touching his face, begging him to open his eyes, but his body lay unconscious. "*Dear God.* Don't die. Please don't die," she half sobbed.

The stallion sensed something was wrong and swung his head back and forth, trying to nudge his master awake.

Rachel didn't hesitate another instant. After mounting Paquita, she broke into a full gallop. Within minutes, she rode in sight of the stable, shouting for help at the top of her lungs.

Almost immediately a dozen workers emerged from various parts of the estate, some already on horseback, not having bothered to saddle up. The solemn group raced with her to the spot where her host still lay inert, his pallor pronounced.

Rachel's heart lurched in her breast and she brushed away the tears streaming down her pale cheeks, terrified he might never wake up.

Everything became a blur as they gently lifted the *señor* from the ground into the arms of one of the stable hands mounted bareback. Rachel rode at his side, her eyes never leaving the *señor*'s beloved face.

To her great joy, as they cantered within view of the stable, her host started to gain consciousness. By the time they reached the back patio where the overwrought housekeeper and staff were assembled, his eyelids fluttered open.

For a brief moment his dark-eyed gaze searched for Rachel and focused broodingly on her, but she couldn't imagine what he was thinking. Then he attempted to stand on his feet without help, evoking a loud cheer from the workers. There could be no more graphic testimonial of the love and esteem in which they held their *patrón*.

Though the women hovered around him, he refused further aid and staggered inside the villa under his own power. Rachel understood the great de Riano pride which would never accept assistance except under the most dire of circumstances and hung back, quietly thanking God for answering her prayers.

After everyone dispersed, she hurried inside and raced up the stairs to get changed and showered before Luisa woke up needing attention.

The rest of the day and evening passed with agonizing slowness because the *señor* had not made a visit to the nursery which was totally unlike him. Her anxiety at a pitch, Rachel cornered Catana who'd brought up the baby's bottle, and demanded news about the *señor*.

According to Catana, he'd been in his apartment since the accident. He'd forbidden the housekeeper to call the doctor and wouldn't allow anyone inside.

That sounded like the headstrong *señor* Rachel had come to adore. What was it Carmen said? That Sharom was the only employee he couldn't intimidate?

Not needing to hear anything else, she put Luisa to bed, then dashed to her room for some shoes. There was no time to change out of her nightgown and robe, let alone tie back her hair which she'd brushed dry earlier after a swim in the pool with Luisa.

Once she'd slipped into a pair of low-heeled sandals, her feet hardly touched the ground as she raced down the mosaic stairway toward the other wing of the house. Relying on instinct, she negotiated the maze of gracefully colonnaded corridors and stairs to reach various parts of the villa which could have belonged to an eastern potentate, though the decor was more subtle and light.

A profusion of flowering plants met her at every turn, filling the balmy night air with the scent of jasmine and rose and a dozen other fragrances which intoxicated her senses. To Rachel, this was the Spain that had a stranglehold on her heart. This memory of the dark-haired *señor* and his home she would take back to New York and cherish in her soul forever.

Please God. Don't let anything serious be wrong with him, her heart cried out as she ran up another flight of stairs to a long hallway where the aging housekeeper stood outside the double doors, wringing her hands and muttering to herself.

Rachel knew exactly how the old woman felt. Everyone loved and revered the *señor,* that much Rachel had learned from living in two Riano households where there were few, if any, secrets.

She'd also learned that the *señor*'s fierce pride would not allow him to exhibit any weakness around the people he loved. But since Rachel didn't belong in that category and was already damned in his eyes, she didn't particularly care what he thought or how he reacted to her interference, not if she could be of help.

The housekeeper crossed herself when she saw Rachel coming. "Did Catana tell you? The *señor* has been hurt, but he will allow no one to attend him. He has locked the door."

Rachel expected as much. Hardening her resolve she said, "Do you have a key to this door?"

The silver-haired woman looked shocked, then a slight gasp escaped and a smile spread over her wrinkled face. She nodded her approval as she took a key from the ring in her apron pocket and handed it to Rachel.

"May the Holy Virgin protect you." She crossed herself once more and hurried off.

Muttering a little prayer of her own, Rachel quietly put the key in the lock and turned it. As soon as she detected the faint click, she twisted the brass handle experimentally and opened the door.

No light relieved the darkness of the room. She hesitated in the entry because she'd never been in this part of the villa before. She assumed that the master bedroom had been built along the same spacious lines as the rest of his palatial-like estate, commanding a sweeping view of the mountains. But that didn't help her now, not when she couldn't see two feet in front of her.

An angry male voice sounded out of the blackness, cursing in volatile Spanish. Rachel jumped in surprise, but was far too relieved to hear him sounding very much the *patrón* to be frightened off. In her fear for his safety, her mind had conjured up visions of finding him on the tile floor, unconscious, or worse....

"Now that I know you're not dead, please speak English, *señor*."

"*¡Madre de Dios!*" she heard him mutter along with a few well-chosen oaths that needed no translation. "How did you get in that door?" he growled furiously, but she heard a betraying note of strain. "I locked it myself hours ago."

"Which was a selfish thing to do when you know perfectly well your staff worships you. Your housekeeper is beside herself with worry. Couldn't you at least have said something to ease her mind?" To Rachel's horror, she could hear a tremor in her own voice. "Surely you must realize that when the king of the castle is under the weather, everyone is upset."

Rachel's temerity must have caught him off guard because a full ten seconds passed before she heard him say, "What's even more surprising is that you could be wrested from Luisa long enough to come and investigate." His mocking retort suffused her face with heat.

Thank heavens for the darkness, she mused inwardly, then experienced utter panic as a light went on.

Its soft, rosy glow fell on the huge bed where the *señor* lay sprawled on his side across the mattress like the savagely beautiful jungle cat she'd once likened him to.

But on that occasion he'd been fully clothed in an elegant linen business suit, whereas now, only a fluffy brown-and-white-striped towel had been hitched about his loins and it looked dangerously loose.

The parts of his body she'd never seen exposed before were as bronzed as his face and neck. The sight of those powerful shoulders and well-defined chest with its matt of black hair left her breathless. Combined with the Moorish and Arabian accents of the room, he put her more strongly in mind of a proud lord of the desert than a Spanish aristocrat.

"Please shut the door and come all the way in, *señorita.*" She did his bidding. "I'm not exactly up to holding court with my staff. But since you're family, I'll make an exception."

Calling on her last vestige of self-control, she tore her gaze from his tautly muscled legs and traversed the length of the room to reach the bed. Belatedly she realized that she'd been so mesmerized by him, she'd forgotten to look for the injury which had brought her to his apartment in the first place.

"I-it's because of Luisa that I decided to take matters into my own hands," she stammered, saying the first thing that came into her head. "She missed her good-night kiss."

Without warning, his hand snaked out and he grasped her wrist, pulling her down onto the bed beside him.

"No. Do not struggle, *señorita*," he commanded when she tried to wriggle away from him. "Even though the accident happened hours ago, the slightest movement makes the world swim."

Instantly she ceased her squirming. "I know what that feels like. Once, when I was in junior high, I was hit in the head by a baseball and suffered a mild concussion. The dizziness didn't go away for several days. I-is there a lump where your stallion kicked you?"

Her question came out in a shaky whisper because he'd pulled her body toward him so they both lay facing each other. The warmth pouring off him, mingled with the scent of soap he'd used in the shower reached out to envelop her, filling her senses with his essence.

While her right arm was crushed beneath her, he had hold of her left. "Feel right here," he whispered back in a tone as husky as hers. The next thing she knew he'd guided her hand to a bump at the side of his head, reminding her of that moment when he'd forced her to touch him, but his black curls hid the nasty wound from view.

She closed her eyes, afraid to look at him, and gently felt the swelling with her fingertips. Even the slightest touch sent a tremor through his body she could feel to her bones. "I—I'm sorry if I hurt you. It's my fault the accident happened at all. Please forgive me. I-if anything more serious had happened, I—"

"You what?" he demanded in a thick toned voice.

"N-nothing. You n-need an ice pack."

"I need many things," he murmured, sounding sluggish. Rachel knew he had to be in a bad way to admit to any vulnerability.

When she dared another peek at him, she noticed the unnatural pallor beneath his hard cheekbones, the slightly bruised look around his eyes which were shut against the pain. As soon as she left the room, she'd phone for the doctor herself.

"I'll bring you some ice, but you'll have to let me go. When I get up, I promise to be careful not to jar you too much."

Suddenly his hand moved to the back of her head and he brought her much closer, sending her heart crashing against her ribs. "Before you rush away, give Luisa this kiss for me."

In the next breath his mouth closed over hers, smothering her tiny cry of surprise.

No matter how many times she'd dreamed, longed for this moment, nothing could have prepared her for the taste of him, for this yielding feeling of delight as he forced her lips apart and began drinking deeply from her mouth.

Rachel could no more stop her response than she could stop breathing. Forgetting everything else, including the reason that had brought her to his room, she began kissing him back with breathtaking urgency, needing the sensations only he could arouse, never wanting this ecstasy to stop.

Without knowing how it happened, she found herself practically lying on top of him, her arms around his neck, her long blond hair in total disarray, some of the golden strands trapped between his marauding fingers.

"*¡Por Dios,* Rachel!" he murmured feverishly against her tender throat where a little pulse throbbed in the hollow.

The sound of his voice penetrated the euphoric haze that held her in thrall. Instantly contrite, she tried to pull away from him but his arms held her fast.

"Forgive me for hurting you, *señor.* I'm afraid it's all I ever manage to do," she lamented, ashamed of her wanton behavior, the total disregard for his injury. In the heat of the moment she'd lost all sense of her surroundings, of decency, and had probably exacerbated his pain and dizziness.

"Look at me, Rachel," he commanded, forcing her to do his bidding. He shook her with surprising strength, his black eyes smoldering dangerously. "You hurt me when you insist on calling me *señor.* My name is Vincente. I want to hear you say it."

If he'd been halfway conscious earlier, he'd have heard her screaming his name so the whole mountain reverberated.

She swallowed hard. "V-Vincente," she finally murmured. It was heaven to do so. "Now please let me go so I can bring help."

She felt his chest heave and suspected his barely suppressed emotions were as raw as hers. "If you truly want to help me, then stay the night with me."

The primitive longing in his voice wrapped around her body like the length of a silken whip.

Dear God.

"I want you, *pequena*," He pressed his mouth to hers again, gently caressing its swollen contours, igniting her desire once more. "I've wanted you for a very long time, and I know that you want me.

"If I had not been so carried away by your sweet innocence and beauty to the point that I foolishly cried out my need of you, we would be satisfying our great hunger for each other right now, instead of just talking about it."

"Our great hunger?" she cried out in alarm.

"*Sí.*" He purred deep in his throat. "If you could see your eyes in the throes of passion, you would know. They speak to mine with a language all their own. Like great purple stars, they explode into hundreds of tiny fragments, each one full of light.

"And your mouth, so exquisitely formed." He traced the trembling outline with his finger until she felt faint from his touch. "It searches continually for mine, restless and questing because no kiss is long enough to satisfy the ache, is it, *pequena?*"

"Don't! Oh, please, don't!" she begged when his hand slid over her robe to settle against her heart, trapping its beat in his palm.

His mouth hovered over hers, his breath sweet against her lips. "Don't you know you can hide nothing from me? Certainly not this vital organ shouting to me that my caresses bring you alive with the slightest brush of my fingers against your velvet skin. Let me make love to you." His voice shook like a man holding on to the last vestiges of control, undermining her pitiful resistance.

"Let me hear you cry out your need of me. I want you in my bed all night long. Be kind to me in my condition, *amorada*. I've been empty for so long.... Don't refuse me, and deny us both paradise," he importuned against her mouth, whispering endearments while she was once again consumed by the fire of his kiss.

This was no dream.

Vincente was actually crushing her in his powerful arms, devouring her with a savage hunger she could never have imagined, not even in her wildest fantasies.

Leonora had known what it felt like to be possessed by him and experience this kind of rapture which had resulted in a baby. She'd been his wife and had a legal and moral right to his love and protection for the rest of their lives.

The realization that he'd only spoken to Rachel of needs and wants, not love, not commitment, filled her with pain, followed by a terrible envy for what she would never have. Vincente was lonely and missing his wife. Rachel was a convenient substitute, nothing more....

She groaned in agony and tore herself from Vincente's possessive hold, sliding off the bed and getting to her feet on shaky legs.

He protested her escape and groped for her, trying to sit up, but the dizziness obviously made him too unsteady and he slumped against the mattress, letting out another smothered imprecation.

But for his injury, he would never have allowed her to leave his bed, not when he knew how desperately she wanted to make love to him, to be loved by him.

Shame swept over her in hot waves, shame that he could so easily unveil her secrets and expose her for the lovesick idiot she was. Without wasting another second, she raced across the floor to the double doors, her only thought to get away.

"That's right," he called out in that mocking voice he generally reserved for her. "Like the innocent, blond Sabine women who ran through the fields from their captors, flee for your life, *pequena.*"

She reached the hallway and shut the doors against his devilish laughter, so out of breath she had to stand there and drink in gulps of air. Injured or not, he would always have the power to tie her emotions in knots.

"*Señorita* Ellis?"

Rachel whirled around, mortified that the housekeeper had been standing in the hallway. How much had the older woman heard? Worse, what must she be thinking?

A glance at her watch indicated she'd been in his room for over an hour, too long for the housekeeper not to suspect that something was going on.

In a jumble of words Rachel explained, "I don't think his wound is too serious, but he needs an ice pack to bring down the swelling. If he's still dizzy in the morning, then call for the doctor."

"I'll get the ice for you."

Rachel averted her eyes. "I—I think it would be best if *you* take it to the *señor.* I've been away from Luisa too long as it is."

The older woman's brows knit into a frown as Rachel pulled the key from her robe pocket and handed it back.

"If that is your wish, *señorita*."

"It is."

Taking a steadying breath Rachel hurried down the long corridor with the resolve that she would leave for New York in the morning. Felipe could drive her to the airport in Seville.

As for Luisa, Carmen would be back any day, and until that time, Catana could watch over her. Rachel had stayed in Spain too long and needed to go home. She had to get far away from Vincente. Her time with him was over.

Everything is over, her heart cried out painfully as she fled down the steps, distancing herself from the source of her pain, aware of the housekeeper's raisin eyes following her progress with blatant disapproval.

CHAPTER NINE

RACHEL'S SYSTEM was too shot with adrenaline to go to bed, let alone to sleep.

After dressing in the skirt and blouse she planned to wear on the plane, she started packing. Once that was accomplished, she straightened the room and put her bags just inside the door to carry down in the morning.

Leaving a brief note on the dresser thanking the *señor* for his hospitality, she headed for the nursery where she spent the rest of the night reliving haunting memories while she rocked the sleeping infant in her arms.

At seven, Luisa awakened with a yawn, then gave Rachel such a sweet smile, Rachel nuzzled her little neck still smelling of baby powder and quietly sobbed. With each passing day, Carmen's daughter resembled Brian a little more, a fact which compounded Rachel's pain.

"Señorita Ellis? I've brought the *niña* her bottle."

Steeling herself to follow through with her plan, Rachel stood up and handed the baby to a surprised Catana.

"Will you please give Luisa her bath and then feed her? I'm leaving this morning." The maid's dark eyes rounded in shock but Rachel was determined, and asked the younger woman if she'd seen Felipe.

"He is not here."

"You mean he has driven the *señor* to work already?" Rachel cried out in consternation. "The *señor* shouldn't be out of bed until he has fully recovered."

Catana hunched her thin shoulders in bewilderment.

Rachel knew she'd get nothing more out of the maid and thanked her. Refraining from kissing Luisa one more time for fear she would lose her resolve, Rachel literally ran out of the nursery, grabbed her purse and bags and started down the hall toward the stairs. Jorge could drive her.

Just as she reached a pair of hand-carved doors leading onto the patio at the rear of the villa, she heard a voice from behind say, "Like a thief in the night, you sneak out of my house without so much as a whisper of goodbye."

Vincente.

Rachel gasped and stopped in her tracks.

Her first thought was that he must be feeling a good deal better. Last night he couldn't sit up in bed, let alone get this far from his apartment. The knowledge that he was able to walk on his own relieved her of a heavy burden.

But his quiet anger was more frightening than all the Spanish epithets at his command.

"Please don't try to stop me from leaving," she said defensively, still afraid to turn around and face him. She didn't dare.

"Since you refused to share my bed last night, it hardly follows that I would wish to detain you this morning. No doubt you will damn me for confessing that I've never had to beg a woman for her favor before. Even more unflattering is the fact that despite my experience with women, such as it is, I could not entice you to lie with me."

Rachel couldn't believe what she was hearing. He had the maddening ability to twist everything she said until she always managed to come out feeling the culprit. Surely he knew the reason she'd run from his arms— Not one word of love had he spoken to her! Not one!

"You're free to go, *señorita*. In fact, I will drive you to the airport myself."

"Where is Felipe?"

"This is his day off."

Rachel had trouble catching her breath. "Then perhaps Jorge can take me. You shouldn't be driving yet. Last night—"

"*¡Basta!*" The stinging lash of his tone made her flinch. "Last night is a subject I prefer not to discuss."

"But you couldn't be well enough to drive!" she blurted out and whirled around, her anxiety over his condition too great to contain any longer.

At first glance, she could see shadows beneath his veiled black eyes, emphasizing his dark Latin face. His hard, yet sensual mouth curved in a devilish twist as her gaze wandered compulsively over the rest of his masculine physique. She tried in vain not to notice how the olive-toned shirt tucked carelessly into hip-hugging jeans molded his well-honed body like a hand in a perfectly fitted kid glove.

Once, in her youth, Rachel and her friends had stood too close to a building which had caught on fire. The intense heat of the exploding inferno forced everyone back.

Standing this close to Vincente felt no different. Tongues of flame darted out to lick at her, singeing her where they touched, consuming her bit by bit until she felt her own body ignite and start to burn out of control.

"Are you in such a hurry that you cannot share a civilized breakfast with me before you go?"

Without gaining her consent, he moved like lightning and relieved her of her bags. After setting them aside, he grasped her elbow in an impersonal gesture and escorted her through the doors to the patio where the rose-scented air was still warm, but not uncomfortably so.

"There's the matter of your salary," he explained, helping her to the table. "If you will give me the name of your bank in New York, I will see that funds are deposited into your account immediately, in American dollars, of course."

"I don't want your money!"

Rachel's outburst coincided with the arrival of one of the kitchen maids who hesitated before bringing rolls, fresh fruit, and coffee to the table. At a brief nod from the *patrón,* she continued with her task, then darted off again.

Drawing in her breath Rachel said, "You've given me room and board while I've been here, plus the opportunity to get acquainted with my little niece. For that privilege alone, I feel I ought to pay *you*. I couldn't take your money." She almost choked getting the words out.

"Nevertheless you shall have it. One of my solicitors can obtain the desired information and see that the transaction is carried out."

"I won't spend the money, so it will be a wasted effort on your part."

"*¡Mierda!*" Suddenly he threw the napkin on the table and pushed himself away from the table with too much force. It sent the scalding hot coffee flying and some of it splashed on Rachel's bare arm, making her wince.

"*¡Madre de Dios!*" This time his imprecation of disgust appeared to be aimed at himself. Before she could countenance it, he'd reached for a nearby watering can and started soaking her arm with a drenched napkin.

"I meant no harm, *pequena,* I swear it." His voice came out rough and unsteady, as if he were in the throes of bitter turmoil.

"I-it was my fault. I insulted you without meaning to. I—I'm sorry."

"You have a way of pressing the thorn into my skin. Too often, you draw blood."

And what do you think you do to me? her soul answered in torment.

He'd gone down on his haunches to minister to her needs. She stared at his downbent head with all that luxuriant black hair she'd run her fingers through last night. She wanted, longed to do it again. But the second she felt the familiar caress of his hands on her body, even though it was out of succor rather than passion, she was lost.

Her eyes closed tightly, and it was all she could do not to cry out her love, to beg him to go on touching her, to hold her captive and never let her go.

"Rachel?"

Unbelievably, it was *Carmen's* alarmed voice which broke through the tension enveloping them, causing Vincente to mutter something unintelligible beneath his breath. "*¿Tío?* Is something wrong?"

Rachel jerked her arm from his hands and got to her feet. She was so shocked by the younger woman's unannounced arrival, so embarrassed to be caught like this because she didn't know what kind of a construction Carmen might put on the scene, that in her haste, she knocked over her chair.

Thanks to the quick reflexes of her host, he prevented it from crashing to the floor.

"I—I'm fine," she explained, wondering why Vincente didn't say anything. Nervously, she turned in Carmen's direction. "Some coffee spil—"

But the rest of the words never left her mouth because Carmen hadn't come out on the patio alone.

A man stood at her side with his arm around her waist, a man almost as tall as Vincente, with a man's shoulders and a healthy head of gilt hair, the gift of the Ellis genes.

No more traces of the eighteen-year-old boy remained.

They stared at each other for a long moment, taking full measure of the similarities and the changes. She didn't know whose eyes filled first.

"Brian!"

She flew across the expanse to his outstretched arms, defying gravity to reach him.

"Spanky." He half laughed, half cried his special endearment for her and swung her around and around.

He hadn't forgotten.

Like a dam breaking, tears gushed down her cheeks and she gave way to her emotions while he rocked her in his arms. When they finally pulled apart to take another look, she could see his throat working.

"You're so beautiful," he said in a husky voice full of wonder. "So grown up. *Lord.*"

"You and Carmen aren't exactly unattractive yourselves," she said, finally managing to find her voice. "Otherwise your daughter wouldn't be the greatest beauty in all Anadalusia."

Brian's eyes radiated blue light. "She is, isn't she? That's because she looks like you." Then he sobered and the lines in his face made him look suddenly older.

"I always intended to come back, Spanky. Can you forgive me for leaving? For staying away so long? I didn't want to, but the pain—"

"I know. I went through my own hell trying to recreate a sense of family by tending other people's children. Don't ask my forgiveness. Let's thank God we have each other."

"Carmen told me about Mother." His voice broke. "It's too late to make it up to her." His shoulders shook and it was her turn to comfort him.

"She wanted *your* forgiveness, remember. I'm sure that wherever she is, she's smiling right now."

"Oh, *Lord,* if I could believe that."

"Believe it, Brian, because it's true. And all you have to do to keep her smiling is love Carmen and your baby with all your heart, for the rest of your lives."

"That part will be easy." He hugged her so tight, it almost knocked the wind out of her. Then he let her go and took control of himself.

After an uneasy silence he once more put his arm around Carmen and they approached the *señor* who had been standing like a dark lord outside their little circle, watching the three of them with an unfathomable expression in his intelligent eyes still shadowed by last evening's injury.

If he was in pain or dizzy, he would never let on. His damnable Spanish pride would never allow it, Rachel mused brokenheartedly.

"Señor de Riano, it's long past time for explanations. But just so you won't think the very worst of me, I'd like you to know that Carmen and I were secretly married by the abbot at La Rabida shortly after I came to work for you."

Rachel's quiet gasp drew surprising looks from everyone. "Th-the abbot never let on," she stammered by way of explanation.

"That's because we swore him to secrecy," Carmen said in his defense.

"I'm so thankful you're married." Rachel's emotional outburst rang throughout the patio. But not by the slightest twitch of a muscle did Vincente let on that their news affected him one way or the other.

"I begged Brian to marry me." Carmen spoke up once more, imploring her uncle to understand with those magnificent eyes Brian couldn't stop watching. Love had transformed her brother.

"I knew you would never approve, *Tío*, because Father always expected me to marry Raimundo and you were determined to carry out his wishes. But I never loved him. When Brian and I met, it was love at first sight.

"I didn't know love could be like that. When he wanted to come forward and ask you for my hand, I wouldn't let him because I was afraid you'd keep us apart...." Her voice trailed in the face of the *señor*'s brooding reticence.

Rachel shivered. How well she knew that look.

"I love your niece, *señor*," Brian broke in forcefully. "My plan was to work hard at your plant to earn enough money to get an apartment for us and pay for my studies so I could finish up my degree in languages."

Rachel's spirits soared. "You've been going to school?"

Brian nodded solemnly. "First in Perugia, then in Cádiz. When the abbot learned I could speak Spanish and Italian fluently, he encouraged me to go into teaching. He has taught Latin and Greek as well as the Romance languages and he thinks I'm good enough to become a professor. That's why he sent me to you, Señor Riano, because he knew I needed better wages if I planned to go on for more schooling."

"Mother left you some money, Brian. It's not a lot, but it will help."

"I want to help but you won't let me," Carmen interjected. "You are stubborn, like *Tío.*"

Brian shook his head and addressed the *señor* once more. "Carmen insisted we could live at her house in Seville, but I told her we had to do it my way, or not at all. It was our first quarrel."

Rachel's gaze flew to the *señor*'s and she withstood its speculative penetration. Without conscious thought her chin lifted a little higher as if to say that her brother was still the honorable young man she remembered.

"The second quarrel occurred when news broke out at the plant concerning the thefts," Brian went on explaining. "It took four months of working there before I suspected that someone on the inside was working with my Swedish roommate to steal from you. At the time I didn't say anything because I needed more proof.

"Lars knew that I'd been watching him, that it was only a matter of time before I came forward with information. But he was arrested before I had the opportunity, and of course he implicated me. Which in turn frightened Carmen who by then was expecting our baby."

Every revelation lightened Rachel's heart a little more, but she couldn't tell what her autocratic host was thinking.

"I was frantic with worry over her, particularly because the first doctor we saw told her that her blood pressure was too high, that she'd need careful watching. That's when I told her we were going to discuss everything with you, *señor.*

"There were more angry words between us. Out of fear for her precarious condition, I finally gave in to her pleadings to go to her godparents in Cordoba and work for them until my solicitor had enough solid evidence to exonerate me in court. But I swear on everything that is holy that I went away *only* on the condition that Carmen live with you, *señor,* and visit the doctor every week and take perfect care of herself."

Brian's earnestness moved Rachel to tears. Surely it had moved the *señor,* but he stood still as a statue.

"I thank God that in spite of everything, you loved her enough to see her through her ordeal. She and the baby have thrived in your care, and for that, I'll always be in your debt. Mercifully that time is over and I've uncovered the evidence needed to clear my name." His voice shook. "With your permission, *señor,* I'd like to have a few words with you in private. There's a person in your employ who needs to be brought in for questioning."

Rachel's joy was short-lived when the *señor*'s black eyes suddenly flashed to hers, his expression as enigmatic and aloof as she'd ever seen it.

"Señorita Ellis, what would you prefer? Shall I drive you to the airport now, or would you be willing to take a later flight so I can accommodate your brother?"

"Airport?" Carmen and Brian cried out at the same time, their consternation as great as Rachel's who'd forgotten all about her intention to leave the villa.

The *señor*'s hard mouth broke into a wintry smile. "That's right. Just this morning I discovered that she has made plans to return to the States. Her bags are packed and ready inside the door. *¿Verdad?*"

Carmen's eyes looked wounded. "You were going to leave before I came back?"

"Sí, chica," her uncle answered for Rachel. "It seems she has a compelling reason for returning to New York immediately, one more urgent than seeing to Luisa's needs any longer."

"That's not fair," Rachel protested, then blushed furiously because her private quarrel with Vincente had become public.

"Rachel—" An unhappy-looking Brian rushed over and put his arms around her. "I've been living for this reunion. You can't go yet. Stay another week, at least. We've got six years of catching up to do."

Carmen clapped her hands, drawing everyone's attention. "I have the perfect solution. After Brian has finished his business, the three of us will drive back to Seville with the baby and leave poor Tío Vincente in peace."

Carmen's suggestion was a godsend. Rachel didn't want to be parted from Brian, not when she'd just found him. But after everything that had transpired, she couldn't stay under the *señor*'s roof another day. She loved him too much to stand the strain of pretense any longer.

In a rush of affection, Carmen flung her arms around her uncle, her happiness shining out of her beautiful face.

"You've always been there for me, just like Papa. It's *my* turn to repay you. From here on out, I have a husband to take care of me, which means you can stop worrying. You need to get on with the rest of your life, dearest *Tío*. You need to find a little happiness for yourself. And I don't know anyone who deserves it more."

"Carmen is right, *señor,*" Rachel inserted boldly to fight the pain. "I've seen for myself how devoted you've been to Carmen and Luisa, how hard you've worked to be father and uncle to them while your own heart has been bleeding. Perhaps now would be a good time for *you* to take a vacation."

His rigid body and implacable features should have warned her not to say anything else, but she had to finish this.

"I—I, too, would be remiss if I didn't thank you, not only for your gracious hospitality, but for your willingness to take me on faith and invite me into your home to look after Luisa while I waited for news of Brian.

"She's an angel and I'll never be sorry for the time spent with her. In fact, I miss her so much already that I'm going to go upstairs and look in on her, *if* you don't mind."

His eyes narrowed to slits of black fire. "I am no longer your employer," he rasped. "You may do as you wish, *señorita.*"

With those words he'd sounded her death knell.

"Good luck," she whispered to Brian, kissing him on the cheek. After smiling at Carmen, she hurried through the doors, but not before she heard the *señor*'s wooden voice invite her brother to join him in his study.

Rachel never made it to the nursery. It took all her strength just to reach her apartment before she collapsed on the bed in abject despair.

AFTER THE FURNACE outside, the blissfully cool interior of Seville's art museum brought Rachel a measure of relief.

Brian, who had an afternoon appointment with the chairman of the foreign language department at the university, had just dropped her off in the Mini he'd bought from a fellow student the year before. He planned to pick Rachel up after his interview and they'd finish sight-seeing. Later that evening, he intended to take Carmen and Rachel out for a night of flamenco.

But the mere sound of the word festered the wound that would never heal. She offered instead to tend Luisa so Brian could be alone with his wife. Though they protested, Rachel was adamant. She had no desire to live through that kind of torture again. She couldn't.

Earlier that morning, at Carmen's insistence, brother and sister had gone off on their own for a little private time together, the first since their return from Aracena three days before. By tacit agreement they'd chosen the palace gardens as the perfect ambience to talk about the past and catch up on each other's lives.

But Brian had always been able to read Rachel's mind. It hadn't taken him long to break her down to tell him what was really going on, why she'd refused to let go and enjoy herself for the few remaining days left to her.

For Rachel, the relief of being able to confide in her brother after so many years' separation had acted like a catharsis. Everything had come pouring out in a torrent of emotion-laden words; the pain of their mother's unexpected death, Stephen's betrayal, and of course, the advent of one imposing Spanish grandee into her life.

Before she'd known it, she'd told him the secrets of her heart and he could be in no doubt that she was hopelessly in love with Vincente de Riano. It seemed the Ellis family shared a fatal weakness for the incomparable beauty of dark Spanish eyes and fiery temperaments to match.

With new insight, Brian had promised that neither he nor Carmen would pressure her or interfere with her plans to return to New York. But she was never to forget that she would always have a home with them in Seville, that from here on out he would be there for her, in any capacity. He loved her, and credited her for smoothing the way with the *señor* so he and Carmen could have a joyous future together.

Thank heavens her brother had found the happiness he deserved, Rachel mused as she wandered from one area of the museum to the other.

Though some of the greatest paintings of the Spanish masters were here on loan from the Prado, Rachel was in no mood to appreciate them. She only gave a cursory glance to the room featuring the chefs d'oeuvre of El Greco.

The dark intensity of his backgrounds, the vibrant, often turbulent life and drama that sprang from each canvas, all were too great a reminder of the *señor*'s electrifying personality. Studying them only produced more pain.

Like the remarkable works in front of her, the *señor* had been endowed with those same intangible qualities not possessed by other men, rare qualities that spoke to her soul.

Hating herself for dwelling on him to the point that she couldn't enjoy anything any more, Rachel hastened toward the exit, hoping Brian had returned and was waiting outside for her. But a painting in the last gallery caught her attention and she came to a standstill.

Rape of the Sabine Women.

The helpless victims, pursued by their captors, fled like hunted animals, reminding Rachel of the *señor*'s mocking words as she'd run from his apartment. But unlike the frightened faces in the painting, Rachel's fear stemmed from within herself.

If she had stayed the night in his arms, he would have known how desperately she loved him. Once he had tired of her, the only emotion she would arouse in him would be one of pity. That's why she'd fled.

"The parallel is unnerving, is it not, *pequena?*"

Vincente. Her heart hammered so hard she feared he could hear it.

She wheeled around, on the verge of asking him what he was doing here. But at the sight of his dark, breathtaking masculinity, at the intimate way his black eyes traveled over her face and body, she couldn't seem to find the words. It felt like months instead of days since she'd seen the faintly sardonic curve of his mouth. Even now she could remember the feel of it as he'd kissed her senseless.

"I came into Seville on police business and decided to drop by the house to see my little Luisa, but Maria informed me that Carmen had taken her to visit a friend," he said at last, reading her mind with alarming ease.

"The timing coincided with a call from your brother, telling me he was going to be delayed. Would I mind sending a car for you?" His shoulders lifted with an elegant, if negligent, shrug. "Since I was available, I offered my services."

"That was very thoughtful of you, *señor,* but you shouldn't have come," she stated primly without looking at him. The thought of getting in his car, of going anywhere alone with him, even for the short trip back to the house, made her so frightened and excited, she felt light-headed.

"I-if Brian hadn't arrived within a reasonable length of time, I would have finished my sight-seeing alone and taken a taxi home."

"Except that you're not going home. While you were out, you had a phone call. It seems you have a visitor who is waiting most anxiously for you at the Don Quixote Inn, so I'll drop you off before I leave for Aracena. It's right on my way."

Rachel's shocked gaze flew to his. "What visitor?"

"The man you're going to marry."

"Stephen?"

Too late she realized that people wandering into the gallery had heard her outburst and seemed to find her conversation with the *señor* of more interest than the paintings.

"If he is the manager of the Kennedy Plaza, then yes."

Stephen was *here?* In *Seville?* Rachel couldn't take it. Liz had warned her about him, but he'd been so far removed from Rachel's thoughts she'd forgotten about him. In fact, she was having difficulty remembering that he'd ever existed. Apparently he had no scruples....

"I—I'm deeply sorry you had to be inconvenienced again, *señor.* Please accept my apologies. I'll get my own ride to the hotel."

She swept past him to reach the entrance to the museum, praying there would be a taxi out front waiting. But he caught up with her and grasped her arm, muttering an imprecation whose tone made her blush even though she couldn't understand the words.

She was forced to exit the door with him and they walked past a cue of taxis to his Lagonda parked around the corner. It reminded her of that other time when he'd been following her from Carmona and given her no choice but to accompany him home.

Unlike before, however, once she was locked inside the car, he didn't immediately turn on the motor and she started to panic.

"You have no right to accost me in a public place and abduct me like a common criminal."

"You gave the right when three nights ago, of your own volition, you entered my bedroom and allowed me to make love to you."

Fire scorched her cheeks. "You know why I came to your room and we did not make love!"

"If by that, you mean we did not finish what you started when you appeared like a golden apparition with your flowing hair and luminous purple eyes, then I agree with you," he returned smoothly.

"But we were most definitely making love to each other the way we've been wanting to do from the very first moment we saw each other. And if I had not been robbed of my strength to the point that I could not move one centimeter without the world spinning, I would not have allowed you to escape and we might still be in my bed experiencing rapture."

"That's not true!" Her voice shook because he'd put voice to the same private, intimate thoughts haunting her.

Ignoring her remark he demanded, "Was it a last minute attack of conscience that drove you out of my arms? The image of the nights you'd spent with your fiancé th—"

"*Fiancé*—" Rachel cried, not waiting to hear the rest. "Stephen was never my fiancé."

She heard a sharp intake of breath and felt his body stiffen before he started up the engine and they took off like a jet stream, passing one car after another as if they were in some kind of concours.

Momentarily stunned by the news and the *señor*'s erroneous assumptions, Rachel had no words and clung to the armrest because he took a corner too fast, causing the tires to squeal. Much to her relief, he finally slowed down as they entered the heart of the city where the late afternoon traffic was atrocious.

"Though I don't condone your lover's tactics, I can understand how he was driven to fire you to bring you to your senses." Another burst of undecipherable Spanish escaped his lips. "Apparently you left New York after your quarrel without giving him a chance to explain anything."

"Thank you for presenting such an eloquent case, *señor*. If I didn't know better, I would assume you were one of Seville's top solicitors. One brief phone conversation and you know all the facts. Carmen was right," she declared, driven over the edge. "You are impossible!"

His hand snaked out to grip hers, clasping it hard enough to still her trembling fingers, revealing the depth of his rage. She was certain that if she tried to pull away, he would apply even more pressure.

"An understanding between two people is binding. In my country, a ring is not necessary to—"

"We're not talking about *your* country!"

She snatched her hand back, too shaken by the touch of his thumb against her palm to withstand it another instant.

"I'll admit there was a time when I had considered marrying him, but—"

"But your worry over Brian prevented the marriage from taking place. Now that he's been found, it seems there's nothing to stand in the way of your happiness."

A bitter laugh escaped. "If you say so. Now please let me out of the car," she demanded because they'd pulled up in front of the high-rise hotel.

After a silence fraught with tension she heard the click that allowed her her freedom. *It was the last thing she wanted.*

Struggling not to break down she said, "For what it's worth, I will always be in your debt for forgiving Brian and accepting him in Carmen's life. *Adieu, se-ñor.*"

CHAPTER TEN

"WHAT DO YOU MEAN it's over?"

Rachel eyed Stephen squarely across the table where they'd been talking the last few minutes. For privacy they'd been placed behind a cluster of date palms which filled the gardenlike foyer.

He looked like any one of a dozen attractive blond Americans sight-seeing in Spain. She felt less than nothing for him.

A waiter appeared and took their order for rolls and coffee. When he left, she said, "Liz warned me you might come to Spain. I didn't believe her and I sincerely wish you hadn't," she said in a quiet voice. "While I've been here, I've learned something very important. I'm not in love with you."

He shook his head in denial. "I don't accept that."

"You're going to have to," she countered. "For what it's worth, I forgive you for everything that has happened. We spent some enjoyable times together and I'll always be grateful for your support after Mother died, particularly when I was so frantic about Brian. But the truth is, you don't love me, either.

"No—" She put up a hand when he started to protest. "When you really love someone, it isn't within the realm of possibility to hold back your feelings, o-or to want anyone else."

She averted her eyes to hide her thoughts of the exciting man who had colored her world for all time.

Stephen was quiet so long, she wondered if he'd heard her. After the waiter had brought them their order, Stephen stared at her, his green gaze accusing. "Are you saying that you've met a man you actually *want?*"

She sipped her coffee, choosing her words carefully. "I'm saying that my feelings for you have never been strong enough to want to go to bed with you. And your feelings for me aren't strong enough to remain faithful. We both deserve the chance to find true fulfillment."

Unfortunately, the only man alive who could make her that happy would never be available to her.

"You *have* met someone!" he said scathingly.

Her jaw hardened, as much from his perception as from his weak character which could turn him into someone she didn't like or know.

"Even if I had, it would do me no good. I'm planning to return to the States soon, and I'll be looking for a new job, one that doesn't involve watching after other people's children. So I won't be needing a reference from you after all."

After tending Luisa, Rachel discovered that the only child she wanted to care for was her own, hers and Vincente's. Since that was out of the realm of possibility, she would find work in another area, even if it meant going back to school while she was on the job.

In fact, the idea of furthering her education appealed a great deal, anything to help her try to forget a certain imposing Spanish lord.

Anger ruddied his cheeks. "It's that bastard, Riano, isn't it?" All pretense at civility was gone in a flash. "King Juan Carlos doesn't have a patch on the arrogant swine. He couldn't get rid of me fast enough on the phone. No doubt he didn't have to beg to get you in his bed."

It was on the tip of her tongue to remind Stephen that apart from herself, he'd never had to beg a woman to sleep with him, either. Women would always flock around him. But such a remark would only make the confrontation uglier.

"I think you've said enough."

Putting down the coffee cup, she got to her feet, unwilling to let him make a scene because his pride couldn't handle rejection or criticism of any kind. He'd behaved like that on the job, retaliating when he couldn't get his own way. She'd tended to close her eyes to his less than desirable traits. *But no longer, grace al señor.*

"Where are you going?"

"That's none of your business. Not anymore. Goodbye, Stephen."

Relieved to have ended it, she walked out of the hotel and took a taxi back to the mansion. To her surprise, Carmen was anxiously waiting for her.

"Rachel! I'm so happy to see you!" she cried out emotionally, hugging her hard.

"I'm happy to see you, too." Rachel shook her head. "Carmen, what's going on?"

"It's the message from *Tío*. He said something about you joining your fiancé at his hotel, and that we shouldn't expect you back to tend Luisa. He said that in all probability you'd be leaving for New York with him. Sharom said *Tío* was in so foul a mood after the call from your fiancé came through, all the servants fled his presence until he stormed out of the house in a rage."

Rachel trembled in reaction. *How dared he put his faulty assumptions to paper and upset everyone!*

"Carmen, you know your uncle. He has this tendency to jump to conclusions before he knows the whole situation. It's true that Stephen came to see me, but by now he's at the airport waiting to board a flight back to New York. It's been over between us since I came to Spain."

"Because of *Tío*. *¿Verdad?*" Carmen's black gaze pierced Rachel's armor. "You love him. I know you do."

Rachel's breath caught. "I swore Brian to secrecy."

"My husband hasn't said a word."

"Then I must be transparent."

Carmen's mouth broke into a breathtaking smile. "To everyone but *Tío*. He's mad with jealousy."

For a moment Rachel's heart leaped for joy, but then she shook her head. "No, Carmen. He couldn't possibly be jealous when he's still grieving for his wife."

Her delicately arched brows met together in a frown. "Where did you get an idea like that?"

"Hernando Vasquez confided that to me the night we went to the Malaguena."

"Hernando is a little blind, like all men. If *Tío* were still in mourning, do you honestly believe he would have pursued you and invented a reason to get rid of me so he could keep you all to himself?"

Rachel blinked in shock. "What are you saying?"

"Simply that *Tío* knew that *I* knew where Brian was hiding, though we never said as much to each other. But he only allowed me to join my husband after you miraculously appeared at the villa. The French call it a *coup de foudre*. Love at first sight. It happened that way for Brian and me, too. Rachel, there's something else you need to know," she said in an urgent tone.

Rachel listened with pounding heart, wanting to hear all of it, but afraid to believe any of it.

"*Tío* was in an arranged marriage. Though he felt a deep fondness for Leonora, it was never love, not the kind he feels for you. If you could see the way his eyes devour you whenever you're not watching, you would begin to understand the strength of his feelings. Go to him! He's the most wonderful man in the world." With a tremor in her voice Carmen added, "*Tío* desperately needs and deserves to be loved by a woman like you."

The blood pounded heavily in Rachel's ears. She stared at Carmen. *What if you're wrong?* she cried inwardly.

"I'm not, you know." Carmen read her mind with uncanny accuracy.

Moistening her lips nervously Rachel whispered, "Will you and Brian drive me to Aracena tonight?"

Carmen slipped her arm around Rachel's waist and hugged her. "The minute he comes through the door."

WITH A SENSE of déjà vu, Rachel alighted from the car at the back of the villa where the sound of chirping crickets filled the summer night air.

The sun had long since dipped below the horizon, outlining the undulating silhouette of the surrounding mountains. Rachel felt the heat still rising from the earth, permeating her senses with the sweet fragrance of roses and honeysuckle coming from the garden, causing her body to ache with unassuaged longings, even to the palms of her hands.

Brian didn't give her a chance to change her mind. The second the door closed, he backed the car out of the drive and headed for Seville, leaving her stranded. Rachel stood alone clutching her overnight bag for dear life before making her way to the back patio.

The *señor* could be anywhere so she moved gingerly, her heart in her throat. For once no staff milled about to acknowledge her presence. The entire villa appeared to be deserted.

Using the key Carmen had given her, Rachel unlocked the back door and slipped inside, almost expecting to hear the *señor* doing laps in the pool, but only a mystifying silence greeted her ears.

Perhaps her host had given his staff the night off. Maybe he wasn't even here. She should have checked the garage before letting Brian and Carmen drive away.

Functioning on pure instinct, she moved through the near darkness toward his apartments. Her breath caught when she saw a spoke of light slanting across the tiles from his suite. He was here.

She approached the entry on tiptoe and peered inside. Her eyes narrowed on his powerful physique still dressed in the same suit he'd been wearing at the museum. However, he'd removed his coat and tie, and his shirt had been pulled loose and hung open to reveal the matt of black hair on his chest.

To her chagrin she'd caught him in the process of packing a suitcase which lay open on the bed. *Where would he be going at this time of night?* she agonized.

"Señor?" she called out softly, wondering at her own temerity, but she loved him too much to run away now.

At the sound of her voice he rapped out something in a dismissive tone, clearly angry to have been disturbed, and continued removing clothes from his dresser. She realized that he thought she was one of the maids....

Setting down her overnight bag, she stepped into his room and shut the door. The click drew his attention. When he saw who it was, his head reared back and his face went ashen, much as it had done after the stallion had kicked him.

His hands stilled and his eyes became angry pinpoints of light. While she waited, perspiration formed on her brow. It seemed an eternity before he spoke.

"Since I, more than any man, know that you'd rather die than cross my threshold a second time, I can only assume you have a very good reason for trespassing on private property, *señorita,*" he said in a wintry voice. "Say what you have to say and then get out!"

The cruelty of his words almost debilitated her. She hadn't expected a welcome, but she never dreamed he could be this forbidding and unapproachable.

"Now that Brian and I have been reunited, we've discovered that we don't want to be apart again, so I—I've decided to make my home in Spain."

His features looked chiseled from granite and his remoteness terrified her. But if she stopped now, she knew she'd never find the courage to face him again.

"The problem is, he and Carmen are still newlyweds and I feel rather in the way. Do you think you could let me stay here for a while? Since I know you'd be offended if I offered to pay for my own room and board, I was hoping we could work out a little different arrangement."

Her explanation managed to stun him. Finally she heard him mutter, "Not five hours ago I left you at the Don Quixote with the man who flew across the Atlantic to claim you."

"Four hours and forty minutes ago I told him I wasn't in love with him and said goodbye. I assume he's on his way back to New York by now."

Forming his hands into fists, he growled, "Don't lie to me, Rachel."

"I may not have always told you the whole truth, but I've never lied to you."

She could hear his mind working out the veracity of her declaration. Then he asked something totally unexpected. "How did you get here?"

"Brian and Carmen drove me. She let me borrow her key to the back door."

He rubbed the back of his neck absently, displaying a rare vulnerability that caught at her heart. "Where are they now?"

"I would imagine they're on their way back to Seville. I—I'm sorry if I've inconvenienced you again, especially when it looks as if you're about to leave on a trip."

"If you weren't in love with him, why did you run from my bed?"

The ferocity of his question excited and terrified her. That as much as anything gave her her first glimmer of hope.

"I—I was afraid."

His black brows furrowed in a menacing line. "*Who* frightened you? Your former lover?"

She shook her head, but he was past reasoning and took another step toward her. "Did he abuse you?"

"No."

"Tell me the truth, Rachel." His chest heaved.

"I am."

"I don't think so. The day we went riding, I wanted you so badly I had to force you to touch me," he said in self-deprecation. "Is he the reason why you've never been able to reach out to me?"

"No!" she cried out in exasperation. "You don't understand. Stephen was never my lover."

A sharp intake of breath broke the silence. "Say that again."

She hugged her arms to her waist. "I've never been to bed with any man."

His gaze narrowed on her classic features for endless seconds before he muttered an imprecation. Now it was his turn to shake his head. "Don't you know I would never hurt you..."

"Not physically anyway," she said in a tremulous voice. The moment the words were out, she knew she'd said the wrong thing.

"*Dios—*" He raked his hands through his hair like someone demented. "What in the name of all that's holy is *that* supposed to mean?"

It was now or never. "I may not have made love before, but I'm not naive to the mechanics. Unfortunately, I believe that for most men, that's all it amounts to, something mechanical and temporary until a new distraction comes along. Love doesn't enter into it."

A piteous expression crossed over his handsome face. "Your father did his damage, didn't he."

"To my mother, yes. But I'm afraid it's *you, señor,* who has taught me life's most painful lesson."

That famous de Riano arrogance slipped into place like a piece of Castilian battle armour. "Explain yourself, *señorita.*"

Holding her breath she asked, "Why is it you never asked me to sleep with you until the night I came to your room uninvited?"

He didn't answer right away, staring at her as if he couldn't quite believe what he was seeing or hearing.

"It's strange how a man like you, who demands total, bald honesty from everyone else, seems to have so much trouble being honest with yourself. So I'll help you."

The dangerous glitter in his eye should have warned her to go carefully.

"Admit you were lonely and hurting, missing your wife. The night blurred the edges and I was there, a convenient substitute for a few hours, perhaps for as long as I remained under your roof.

"No—" She held up her hand when he would have come closer. "No doubt most women would be over-joyed to have even that much of you, and consider themselves blessed. But I'm not most women." Her voice cracked, breaking down fast. "I'm too greedy for that. I want it all— Forever!" she blurted out, her heart pounding wildly.

He groaned her name.

"Let me finish, please. You see, I never knew what it was to truly desire a man in all the ways that really matter, not until I first laid eyes on you. You wouldn't believe the fantasies I've had about you, even the one where you threw me down on the cold marble floor and ravished my slender, pale body," she admitted, re-minding him of the comment he'd made that day in his study. "The truth is, I'd dreamed of it happening long before the words ever left your lips.

"I-if this is how Carmen felt when she met my brother, then I can understand why she defied even you to have her heart's desire."

He said something she couldn't understand because she was too caught up in her own overwhelmed emotions.

"The truth is, there's simply no one to compare to you, *señor,* and there never will be again, a-and I couldn't bear the thought of being your comfort for one night, and then forgotten. It would destroy me.... That's why I ran away."

She lifted her eyes to him, pools of liquid light turned purple from the depth of her passion. "Do you have any idea how jealous I've been of your attentions to Luisa? Every second that you are with her, I watch you kissing her neck, murmuring tender endearments against her skin, holding her next to your heart.

"And Carmen— She has the right to throw her arms around your neck any time of the day or night and tell you how much she loves you. She thinks you're the most wonderful man in the world, and you are." Her voice throbbed.

"Everyone adores you, worships you. But no one will *ever* love you the way I do. *No one.*" The room reverberated with her passionate avowal. "It hurts how much I love you," she cried in literal pain.

"Shall we talk about hurt, *señorita?* About pain?" he returned emotionally, his body trembling. "Shall we talk about the times when you told me you hated me, that I was a throwback to the Middle Ages, that you were disappointed when it was I, and not your brother, who followed you from Carmona?"

Suddenly Rachel was lifted from the ground and brought up against his heart, her face buried in his neck while he crushed her in his arms. "Shall we catalog the wounds inflicted by your rapier tongue, *amorada?* Wounds that left me dazed and bleeding?"

She felt his great body shake from emotion and couldn't believe it was her darling Vincente holding her as if his very life depended on it.

"Never have I met such a woman who wanted *nothing* from me." His voice sounded hollow from remembered pain. "It's a miracle I didn't strangle you with my bare hands after I caught up with you on Paquita riding hell-bent for death. Obviously it was preferable to ending up in my arms."

She nestled closer. "Now you know differently," she whispered against his neck, thrilling to the freedom of loving him like this.

"But you administered the coup de grace when you ran terrified from my bed. Your feet never touched the ground in your haste to escape me. *Dios.*"

"Y-you still haven't told me what I'm dying to hear, *señor.*"

"You mean 'love.' Love is a very strong word, a word you Americans use to describe every emotion you feel, from your interest in a basketball game to your fondness for apple pie. We Spaniards are more selective and reserve such an important word for the moment when we find our true soulmate. For many unfortunate people that moment never comes, not even in an entire lifetime."

Shattered by this new insight into his psyche, Rachel hugged him around the waist, trying to cope with the pain.

"So Hernando was right."

"Hernando?" He lifted his head from her hair and forced her to look up at him. "What does he have to do with this conversation?" She hid her face. "Answer me!"

"H-he said your heart was buried with Leonora. But Carmen sai—"

"Listen to me this one time, *amorada,*" he broke in without hesitation, "then we need never discuss it again. I cared for Leonora in my own way. Our families were very close and our marriage was planned long before she and I decided that our easy friendship made us compatible enough to live together and raise a family."

Unable to keep silent she blurted out, "Then are you saying that you've never truly been in love before?"

"No. I'm not saying that."

"Then there is someone else?" Her voice shook.

"Yes, you little fool. I'm holding her in my arms right now. By all that is holy," he began in thick tones, "I swear that what I tell you now, I've never said to another woman. This one time I will say it in your language, then I'll say it in my own for the rest of our lives.

"I love you, Rachel Ellis, from the depth of your constant heart to the purity of your immortal soul. I've loved you from the first moment you appeared on my property, your magnificent eyes a deep shade of violet because of your anxiety over your brother.

"I watched the rays of the late afternoon sun set fire to your gossamer hair. *Dios*—" His voice shook with the force of his emotions. "I wanted to feel the imprint of your beautiful body so intensely that I probably willed that faint to come upon you so I would be allowed to gather you in my arms and achieve my heart's desire."

"I—I wanted to be in your arms every bit as badly," she confessed against his mouth which had started devouring hers. Moaning her need, she gave herself up to the long, pent-up passion which she no longer had to suppress.

Vincente de Riano, the dark, proud lord of her dreams, the secret lover of her most private and intimate fantasies, wanted her, loved her with a depth of hunger she would never have imagined.

When he allowed her to breathe she whispered, "From the second you cuddled Luisa against your shoulder, I've wanted to feel your baby growing inside of me."

"Rachel—"

She silenced him with her lips, her heart so full of love, she wondered if she could die of it. "I've longed to give you a son or daughter who would know your love, your goodness. I've ached to be your wife, to be able to touch you, kiss you whenever I felt like it. You'll never know the agony I've suffered because I thought you couldn't love me."

He shook his head. "When you came back to the villa tonight, I was preparing to follow you to New York and convince you that you loved me and were going to marry me! If you didn't cooperate, I planned to kidnap you and I would have," he vowed with a ferocity that made her shiver because she knew he was telling the truth.

Before she could countenance it, he swept her up in his powerful arms and carried her toward the door. "Wh-where are you taking me? I thought—"

"You do too much thinking," he teased in a way which was achingly familiar. "Right now we're going to pay a call on the abbot. Within the hour he'll be pronouncing the words that make you legally, spiritually, and physically mine.... Señora de Riano, my adored *esposa.*"

He lowered his dark head, his black eyes ablaze for her. "Once we exchange our vows, I am taking you to my bed where you belong. Enjoy the view as long as you can, *pequena,* because I cannot guarantee when you will see the light of day again."

"Vincente—" She gasped as the full meaning of his words filled her soul with inexpressable joy.

"At last you cry my name the way you did one other time. But you left my bed too soon. I've been dying ever since. Only you can bring me back to life," he murmured against her mouth, his kiss of fire leaving her weak and clinging to the man who was about to become her husband.

"Tonight Carmen told me you loved me," she admitted when he allowed her to draw breath.

"Carmen is an intelligent woman and knew exactly how it was between you and me," he said, preempting her in a wry tone. "She purposely announced that the three of you were going back to Seville to leave me in peace. It was her way of exacting revenge because she could see how besotted I was with you, how empty my life would be after you were gone. After all, she'd been through the fatal experience of falling headlong in love with your brother the first moment she met him, too. The Ellis charm is deadly, *pequena.*"

She molded herself even closer to him. "You don't know what deadly is. You would have to be a woman and sustain one fiery glance of your beautiful black eyes to know the true meaning of the word. One look from you and I was lost.

"I adore you, Vincente," she half sobbed. "I'm so much in love with you that I'm terrified this isn't real, that you're only a fantastic figment of my imagination." She hugged him harder, to prevent him from disappearing. "I couldn't live without you now," she confessed in a shaky voice.

"Then let us go and say our vows before God who has blessed us with such a precious gift."

"But it's so late. We'll disturb the abbot."

"I'm afraid he's used to the unorthodox ways of the de Riano family. Carmen confided that he married them in the middle of the night. Our late arrival at the monastery won't come as any great shock."

Her eyes misted over. "Do you have any idea how happy I am?"

To her surprise, a shadow crossed over his features. "I'm warning you now, Rachel. I'll never let you go. Not even if you wake up tomorrow and try to run from my bed because everything is unfamiliar and you wish you were back in America."

She shook her head and cupped his incredibly handsome face between her hands. "You still don't get it, do you?"

His dark brows met in a frown. "*Get it?* What exactly do you mean by that expression?"

He was perfectly serious and her heart experienced another profound surge of love for him. His English was remarkable, but there would always be those elusive idioms found in every language which he hadn't yet learned. This was one of them.

"I think it will be better if we get married first. Then, when I'm your wife, I'll have the right to show you over and over again what I mean, *exactamente*," she teased.

After flashing him a provocative smile she whispered, "Maybe by the time our first child is on the way, my dearest, beloved, headstrong, adorable *señor*—" she kissed his dominant jaw "—you'll begin to understand."

HARLEQUIN ROMANCE®

brings you:

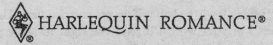

Penny Sullivan moves away to start a new life when her love affair with Reid Branden ends in bitterness—but her young niece unwittingly brings them back together again. Will Penny and Reid's love blossom again—or will the past continue to haunt them?

#3366—P.S. I LOVE YOU by Valerie Parv
June's *Sealed with a Kiss* title

Available wherever Harlequin Books are sold.

In coming months, watch for these exciting
Sealed with a Kiss titles:

July: #3369—*Wanted: Wife and Mother*
by Barbara McMahon
August: #3373—*The Best for Last*
by Stephanie Howard
September: #3378—*Angels Do Have Wings*
by Helen Brooks

Harlequin Romance—Dare to Dream

SWAK-4

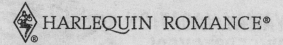

HARLEQUIN ROMANCE®

celebrates

Join us in June for *Family Ties!*

Family...what does it bring to mind? The trials and pleasures of children and grandchildren, loving parents and close bonds with brothers and sisters—that special joy a close family can bring. Whatever meaning it has for you, we know you'll enjoy these heartwarming love stories in which we celebrate family—and in which you can meet some fascinating members of our heroes' and heroines' families.

It all begins with...
**#3365 *Simply the Best*
by Catherine Spencer**

ANNOUNCING THE

FLYAWAY VACATION SWEEPSTAKES!

This month's destination:

Beautiful SAN FRANCISCO!

This month, as a special surprise, we're offering an exciting FREE VACATION!

Think how much fun it would be to visit San Francisco "on us"! You could ride cable cars, visit Chinatown, see the Golden Gate Bridge and dine in some of the finest restaurants in America!

The facing page contains two Entry Coupons (as does every book you received this shipment). Complete and return *all* the entry coupons; **the more times you enter, the better your chances of winning!**

Then keep your fingers crossed, because you'll find out by June 15, 1995 if you're the winner! If you are, here's what you'll get:

- Round-trip airfare for two to beautiful San Francisco!
- 4 days/3 nights at a first-class hotel!
- $500.00 pocket money for meals and sightseeing!

Remember: The more times you enter, the better your chances of winning!*

FLYAWAY VACATION
SWEEPSTAKES
OFFICIAL ENTRY COUPON

This entry must be received by: MAY 30, 1995
This month's winner will be notified by: JUNE 15, 1995
Trip must be taken between: JULY 30, 1995-JULY 30, 1996

YES, I want to win the San Francisco vacation for two. I understand the prize includes round-trip airfare, first-class hotel and $500.00 spending money. Please let me know if I'm the winner!

Name_____

Address _____ Apt. _____

City   State/Prov.   Zip/Postal Code

Account #_____

Return entry with invoice in reply envelope.

© 1995 HARLEQUIN ENTERPRISES LTD.   CSF KAL

FLYAWAY VACATION
SWEEPSTAKES
OFFICIAL ENTRY COUPON

This entry must be received by: MAY 30, 1995
This month's winner will be notified by: JUNE 15, 1995
Trip must be taken between: JULY 30, 1995-JULY 30, 1996

YES, I want to win the San Francisco vacation for two. I understand the prize includes round-trip airfare, first-class hotel and $500.00 spending money. Please let me know if I'm the winner!

Name_____

Address _____ Apt. _____

City   State/Prov.   Zip/Postal Code

Account #_____

Return entry with invoice in reply envelope.

© 1995 HARLEQUIN ENTERPRISES LTD.   CSF KAL

OFFICIAL RULES
FLYAWAY VACATION SWEEPSTAKES 3449
NO PURCHASE OR OBLIGATION NECESSARY

Three Harlequin Reader Service 1995 shipments will contain respectively, coupons for entry into three different prize drawings, one for a trip for two to San Francisco, another for a trip for two to Las Vegas and the third for a trip for two to Orlando, Florida. To enter any drawing using an Entry Coupon, simply complete and mail according to directions.

There is no obligation to continue using the Reader Service to enter and be eligible for any prize drawing. You may also enter any drawing by hand printing the words "Flyaway Vacation," your name and address on a 3"x5" card and the destination of the prize you wish that entry to be considered for (i.e., San Francisco trip, Las Vegas trip or Orlando trip). Send your 3"x5" entries via first-class mail (limit: one entry per envelope) to: Flyaway Vacation Sweepstakes 3449, c/o Prize Destination you wish that entry to be considered for, P.O. Box 1315, Buffalo, NY 14269-1315, USA or P.O. Box 610, Fort Erie, Ontario L2A 5X3, Canada.

To be eligible for the San Francisco trip, entries must be received by 5/30/95; for the Las Vegas trip, 7/30/95; and for the Orlando trip, 9/30/95.

Winners will be determined in random drawings conducted under the supervision of D.L. Blair, Inc., an independent judging organization whose decisions are final, from among all eligible entries received for that drawing. San Francisco trip prize includes round-trip airfare for two, 4-day/3-night weekend accommodations at a first-class hotel, and $500 in cash (trip must be taken between 7/30/95—7/30/96, approximate prize value—$3,500); Las Vegas trip includes round-trip airfare for two, 4-day/3-night weekend accommodations at a first-class hotel, and $500 in cash (trip must be taken between 9/30/95—9/30/96, approximate prize value—$3,500); Orlando trip includes round-trip airfare for two, 4-day/3-night weekend accommodations at a first-class hotel, and $500 in cash (trip must be taken between 11/30/95—11/30/96, approximate prize value—$3,500). All travelers must sign and return a Release of Liability prior to travel. Hotel accommodations and flights are subject to accommodation and schedule availability. Sweepstakes open to residents of the U.S. (except Puerto Rico) and Canada, 18 years of age or older. Employees and immediate family members of Harlequin Enterprises, Ltd., D.L. Blair, Inc., their affiliates, subsidiaries and all other agencies, entities and persons connected with the use, marketing or conduct of this sweepstakes are not eligible. Odds of winning a prize are dependent upon the number of eligible entries received for that drawing. Prize drawing and winner notification for each drawing will occur no later than 15 days after deadline for entry eligibility for that drawing. Limit: one prize to an individual, family or organization. All applicable laws and regulations apply. Sweepstakes offer void wherever prohibited by law. Any litigation within the province of Quebec respecting the conduct and awarding of the prizes in this sweepstakes must be submitted to the Regies des loteries et Courses du Quebec. In order to win a prize, residents of Canada will be required to correctly answer a time-limited arithmetical skill-testing question. Value of prizes are in U.S. currency.

Winners will be obligated to sign and return an Affidavit of Eligibility within 30 days of notification. In the event of noncompliance within this time period, prize may not be awarded. If any prize or prize notification is returned as undeliverable, that prize will not be awarded. By acceptance of a prize, winner consents to use of his/her name, photograph or other likeness for purposes of advertising, trade and promotion on behalf of Harlequin Enterprises, Ltd., without further compensation, unless prohibited by law.

For the names of prizewinners (available after 12/31/95), send a self-addressed, stamped envelope to: Flyaway Vacation Sweepstakes 3449 Winners, P.O. Box 4200, Blair, NE 68009.

RVC KAL